TINY TREE

First Published 2023
Tiny Tree
[an imprint of Andrews Uk Ltd]
West Wing Studios, Unit 166,
The Mall Luton, Beds, LU1 2TL United Kingdom

ISBN: 978-1-913230-35-7

Cover Illustration © Bruna Oliveira Marini

To Kate

DAVID BARKER
PAX
AND THE MISSING HEAD

TINY TREE

To Kate

DAB

PART ONE

THE WORKHOUSE

CHAPTER ONE

Pax stood on the edge of the crumbling, 20th floor balcony with the wind pulling at his orange boiler suit. He'd finished checking the lettuces and now it was tomatoes up on twenty-one. He leant backwards, letting the harness take his weight as he stared up at the sky. He pressed a button on the hand-held controller to wind in the rope and began to walk up the side of the tower. High above, the machine grumbled through its worn-out gears, setting Pax's teeth on edge.

Crunching cog wheels! Bet I could fix that in no time.

Pax loved mending things. He was good at it. It made him feel useful, important. But the Worshipful Company of Engineers wouldn't dream of anyone so young doing their job. So instead, he had to make do with tending the verti-farms and stripping out spare parts from junked electronic kit back in the workhouse.

His reflection flashed at him from window glass as he ascended. A 12-year-old boy in overalls that didn't fit. Slender wrists protruded from the ends of rolled-up sleeves and a length of electrical flex acted as a belt.

Rows and rows of green stalks, bejewelled with ruby red tomatoes, welcomed Pax to the 21st floor. Something had been at one of the plants. He could smell the sweetness before he saw the sticky juice beneath the trellis of fruit, marking the scene of the crime. Peering closer he spotted little paw prints and tiny teeth marks. Definitely not a bird. Pax reached into his backpack and retrieved a couple of traps. They were supposed to be one-way tickets to the great mouse hole in the sky but Pax had rigged his to catch the little pests. Ginger paid more for live specimens, though what she did with them, Pax had never dared to ask.

The great clock at Westminster Palace started to ring out the hour and Pax's fingers went to the back of his head, rubbing the metallic dots that spelled out a serial number. 45B1. Of course, he knew that meant he was born in 2045, the first seedling boy of that year. And yet he couldn't help feeling there was a connection to the Palace clock. Four little bells playing five tunes, before one big bell chimed out.

"45B1? You still only on tomatoes? You can daydream all you like once I'm in the army, but until then, get a move on!"

That was the team leader, 42B6, over the headset. Otherwise known as Charlie, on the west side of the building. And obviously impatient to get back to the dorms. But Pax never hurried. On still days, yellow smog lay over the city like a blanket. Up above it, with just the other verti-farms and the crumbling wreck of the Beattie tower for company, Pax could imagine that he had been transported to a land of dreams and peace. He liked the smell of clean air, it tasted of freedom.

Today, the winds had tugged away the smog and beyond the sea of roofs, Pax could see The Wall on the horizon, a giant ring of steel encircling the capital. A barrier to stop the rich and the old from contaminating the supposed perfection of New London.

Pax spotted movement near one of the towers on The Wall and wondered if it was a drone attack. It had been a few days since the last one, after all. He took out the collapsible telescope he made last year and peered through. No, the movement was too graceful. Just a flock of birds, looking for somewhere good to land, not caring which side of The Wall they were on.

A quick glance at his watch and a gulp. He was definitely behind schedule. Last time he had kept everybody waiting, Commandant Hanson had yelled himself hoarse and given Pax latrine duties for a week. Pax hurried to finish checking the rest of the tomatoes, talking on his headset as he went.

"Why are you so keen to join the Defence Force, 42B6?"

"I'm bored," said Charlie. "Just wait 'til you've been farming for five years. Besides, the grub's better in the Army. Now get a move on."

Pax shook his head.

Rushing off to war? No thank you.

He hurried to the precipice outside and leant back, pressing the up button on his winch before the slack had gone out of the line. A horrible crunching noise erupted from the roof as the rope lost all its tension and Pax started plummeting towards the ground. His stomach took a moment to catch up. Pax wanted to scream but all the air had already left his lungs.

If he could just grasp the controller and squeeze both sides, an emergency brake would halt his descent. But the device was flailing at the end of its short tether. Tears streamed from windswept eyes. He fumbled blindly for the controller as he spun like a gyroscope. He waved his limbs about trying to stabilise the fall. The ground was rushing up to meet him like an express train.

Just in time, his fingers found the trigger and squeezed hard. A pulse shot back up the line and, on the roof, a clamp snapped shut. He folded in half as his waist jerked to a sudden halt, the harness slicing into his stomach and groin. His eyes began watering again for very different reasons.

The descent had come to a halt only a couple of metres short of the ground. Pax wasn't sure whether to whoop with joy or burst into tears. He was too shocked to do either. So instead, he just dangled there, waiting for somebody to come and get him down while his breathing and heart rate returned to normal.

He felt liquid running over his top lip and tasted iron. His fingers confirmed the diagnosis: a nose bleed. He tried to tilt his head forward to avoid getting any stains on his new boiler suit. That would just be another excuse for Hanson to punish him.

Eventually, Charlie appeared from around the corner and tutted. "When I said hurry up, I didn't mean you had to chuck yourself out of a window, Pax."

"Beat you down, though, didn't I?"

CHAPTER TWO

I n a noisy room full of long tables and thin, hard benches Pax and Charlie carried their lunch trays towards a gap in the seating. The heads of workmates bobbed up and down as they ate, their buzz-cut hair showing off the metallic dots at the base of each skull. As usual, there was little joy in the canteen, just murmured conversations and eyes that shifted around the room, like feeding animals on the look-out for predators.

High windows let the midday sun stream in at a steep angle, highlighting the motes of dust. One wall of the dining room was dominated by a huge, charcoal-coloured film of glass. As Pax walked past it, the screen flickered into life. It showed the white, square Tower of London and fluttering from the central turret, a green pennant that bore the emblem of New London: a silver cog and spanner.

Pax and Charlie sat down as the screen switched to a female newsreader behind a desk. She smiled into the camera.

"Welcome citizens to another beautiful morning in New London. Our top story on day 1843 of Silas Letherington's reign as Lord Mayor. Thanks to his wise leadership the mines continue to exceed output targets for this quarter."

Charlie leant over his food to whisper to Pax. "Thanks to his wise leadership? The only thing Old Leathery knows how to do is eat."

"Charlie!" Pax glanced up at the security camera in the corner of the ceiling. "Shh! They might be listening…"

The newsreader continued in the background. "In other news, the head of the Worshipful Company of Bakers was replaced after bread production fell short over the summer."

Charlie sat up straight and rolled his eyes. "Isn't that the third one this year?"

Pax once again glanced nervously towards the camera.

Charlie rubbed at the faint wisps of a beard on his chin, looking down at Pax. "Look, Pax, you know I'm off to join the Defence League soon, right? Why don't you start sitting with the other kids? The ones nearer your age."

Pax stabbed at a lump of something grey on his plate. He pinched his nose and swallowed the morsel whole. "They think I'm weird."

Charlie raised an eyebrow. "I know they tease you, but you could make more of an effort."

"Since that mining accident took the twins..." Pax's heart pinched tight as he remembered them. "You're the only friend I've got left around here." A scuffle broke out in the corner of the canteen as two boys fought over some food. Pax turned away. He hated conflict. Even when the bullies stole his food, he never fought back.

Charlie looked at the ceiling as if he were looking for the right words. "Pax, we make a good team, but that's not friendship. Friends... have things in common, they share jokes."

"I can do jokes. I heard one the other day. Knock-knock."

Charlie sighed. "Who's there?"

"Nobody... No, wait, err... that wasn't it. Umm... I'll try to be more like you, I promise. I'll learn some jokes for next time." Pax stared at Charlie, hoping to see some sign of compromise but was met with a blank face. "Can't you wait it out a bit longer before joining the army?"

Charlie shook his head. "I'm desperate for some proper grub."

"You don't like Rat-a-tailly?" Pax picked up a thin, long strand from his plate. It looked like a piece of spaghetti with hairs on and smelt faintly of the boys' toilets. "Seriously, patrolling The Wall just for better food?"

"A 'zen like me don't got many career options, Pax. Wait 'til you've been farming as long as I have. When all you've got to show for five years of graft is muscles and dirty fingernails, you'll be desperate to get away too."

Before Pax could reply, a gong chimed and everybody hurried to clear their trays away, heading for the exit. Back in the main corridor, he headed left, up the worn wooden stairs with the tramp of boots echoing around the stairwell. On the first-floor landing, Pax turned right, tagging along with eleven other children to the end of a plain corridor. The sign on the wall read 'Tech Recycling Lab, WH5.' Pax entered the room with a smile.

The dozen workstations waiting inside each had a large, illuminated magnifying glass on an adjustable arm and a tray of sharp implements and tiny tools. On the right-hand side of each table, a crate full of old, junked IT and electronic items was waiting to be picked through and on the left an array of small boxes, ready to receive the components worth recycling. Pax hurried to his favourite spot while the others shuffled into the room.

"Well don't just dawdle, children. Your shift has started. Get to work!" Miss Scrubs, in her spotless white boiler suit was their overseer. She glowered down at them from her raised platform at the end of the room.

Pax snapped on his safety goggles and looked at the crate on his desk, pondering which item to choose first. The buzz of a small angle grinder broke the silence. As the smell of melting plastic invaded his nostrils. Pax put on a mask, picked up an old mobile phone with a shattered screen and started to take it apart with surgical precision.

He began to hum a happy tune, ignoring the tuts from others around him. As he disassembled each item, he considered which components might be useful for his own projects. Which ones might be worth filching from under the nose of Miss Scrubs. Today's haul included a pair of yellow LED lights and a half-charged battery cell. Pax worked so quickly, and the heap of old items was replenished so often, it was impossible to tell that not all his recycled components ended up in a sorting box.

11

A girl with curly red hair entered the room and walked up to Miss Scrubs. After a brief whispered conversation, she approached Pax's workstation.

He looked up. "Alright, Ginger?"

"Do you want the good news or the bad first, Pax?"

Pax shrugged, continuing to work on a broken laptop. "Good, I suppose."

She leant forward and whispered. "I'm paying double for any mice you get me this week."

Pax smiled, thinking back to the traps he'd laid earlier that day. "And the bad?"

"Hairy Hanson wants a word with you," her voice suddenly loud again.

Everybody stopped working.

"Me?" Pax looked around the silent room, suddenly conscious of eleven set of the eyes all turning to look at him. His cheeks flushed red. "What... what does he want?"

Ginger shrugged. "He just told me to come get you. Now, chop, chop. Or he might think I was slow in fetching you."

Sizzling circuits!

Pax took off his mask and gloves with shaking hands. The acrid smell of the room stung the back of his throat as he threaded past other workstations towards the door.

"And don't forget those mice," Ginger called after him.

Outside in the corridor, Pax leant against the wall. He wiped sweat off his forehead and took a deep breath. After years of getting away with it, had he finally been spotted stealing recycled items? He scurried towards the central stairs and went up to the second floor.

He walked past the thick-necked security guard, past the portraits of previous workhouse leaders. He tried not to look at McGovern 2049-51, with his drooping moustache and eyes that seemed to burrow into your soul. That picture always gave Pax the shivers. Approaching the Commandant's door, he paused to wipe his hands on the back of his boiler suit and polished each of his boots in turn on the back of the opposite leg. He rapped on

12

the door. Hearing a grunt that sounded like 'Enter' he turned the handle and walked in to meet his doom.

"You, err… wanted to see me, sir?"

"Ahh, four-five-bee-one. Well don't dawdle, boy. Come in. New London is no place for losers."

"We will win," replied Pax. He instinctively banged a fist against his chest and formed a V-shaped victory sign with two of the fingers on that hand, holding them out as Commandant Hanson acknowledged the sign with a small nod of his head.

Pax's steps felt weird as his boots sunk into the thick carpet. The afternoon sun was streaming in through open blinds on the far side of the huge desk. Pax could just make out the silhouette of the Commandant's sprawling hairline and the faint aroma of hair tonic, but couldn't see the expression on his face.

Pax approached slowly, awaiting further instruction. He looked down at the desk, trying to keep the sun out of his eyes. At a swipe of the Commandant's hand the glass screen built into his desk went dark. Pax tried to swallow but his mouth had gone very dry. The silence was ominous.

A hairy finger reached out to press a button on the side of the desk and the blinds snapped shut, blocking the sunlight. Pax felt his heart squeeze tight as he finally saw the wicked grin cracking open the Commandant's beard. There was only one thing that made Hairy Hanson smile: dishing out punishment.

"I hear there was some trouble at Mandela Heights this morning? Hmm? A winch failure?"

Pax released the breath he'd been holding in for too long. "Oh, I'm alright thank you, sir. Just a bit bruised. No harm done."

"No harm done? No harm done, he says!" Commandant Hanson's bushy black mane took on a life of its own as he threw back his head. "You failed to complete your roster. And you damaged a value piece of equipment. Bah!"

Pax stepped backwards, lowering his eyes and hunching his shoulders. "But that winch has been playing up for ages, sir."

"Then you should have reported it earlier. Do you know how long it will take the Engineers to get round to repairing it?"

Pax straightened for a moment. "I could have a go at it myself."

"Don't be ridiculous, boy. A third-rate citizen like you doing Company work? You have ideas above your station." The Commandant swiped a hand across his desk glass and as it came back to life, he manipulated some files, eventually selecting a video clip that played on the flat surface. It showed Pax, enjoying the sun on top of one of the verti-farms. "Last week, a drone spotted you slacking up on the roof for ten minutes at the end of your shift. What have you got to say to that?"

Pax's stomach shrank to the size of a pea as he tried to think of an excuse and not his imminent punishment. "I'm sorry, sir," he finally spluttered. "It was really hot that day, and there's so much to do at this time of year. We'd worked really hard... It won't happen again."

"I know it won't. I'm taking you off the farms. I will not tolerate weakness in Workhouse Five.

Pax winced as if the Commandant had slapped him. Maybe a beating would be preferable to being taken off the verti-farms. No more clean air. No more peace and quiet. And there would be no double payment from Ginger for those mouse-traps if he couldn't go back to collect. He wondered if this day could get any worse.

Commandant Hanson stood up and leant over the table. "I think a stint in the sewers is called for. Bah! Can't cause much trouble down there, hey?"

Ahh, yes, apparently this day could get worse. A lot worse.

CHAPTER THREE

After supper, Pax collapsed back onto his bed, the weight of the day's events pressing down on him. Pushed away by Charlie, pushed down the sewers by Hairy Hanson for ratting duty, as it was known. Even the one thing he liked doing – his session in the recycling lab – had been cut short. As he replayed the horrible events in his head, the quiet of the dorm was broken by chanting, coming from outside the workhouse. Snatches of a protest song drifted in through the high windows of the dormitory.

Pax couldn't quite hear what they were complaining about this time, but usually it was the rationing or the long working hours. People were beginning to wonder if the Great Divide had really been worth it, splitting the country into the Guild of Cities and the Countryside Alliance. Such talk was practically illegal, but it didn't stop the protests. Nobody seemed happy in New London. Even Commandant Hanson with his easy job, plush office and generous food allowance was grumpy most of the time.

The whine of an approaching hover ship drowned out the chants. As soon as the engine powered down, Pax heard boots landing hard on the ground, no doubt belonging to Officers of The Arm – the mayor's enforcers. The sound of the song was replaced by the noise of fighting and screaming. And then silence again.

Pax sighed and checked there was no-one around in the dorm. Most of the kids who weren't working an evening shift were outside in the courtyard, making the most of the late sunset. Reaching into the bottom drawer of his bedside cabinet, he pulled out a cylindrical tin tube with a mounted camera at one end, tiny wheels at the other. As he flicked a switch on its base, Pax felt his heart warm a little and the tension in his shoulders unwind.

This was Bee-Bop, his finest creation to date. It had taken him months of filching and secret work to assemble. He placed the robot on the floor.

"Play me some music, please Bee-Bop?"

The robot's dome whirled around as a little set of multi-coloured light flashed on and off. The wheels whirred into motion as the robot completed a figure of eight on the floor next to Pax's bed and a simple tune began.

Pax smiled. "You'll never leave me, will you?"

But as he said these words, the robot slowed to a stop and all but one of the lights faded. The music ended and, in its place, an electronic voice blurted out of the speaker.

"Pax, we need to talk."

It was Alderman – the super computer that helped run New London. "Alderman? What have you done?" Pax couldn't bear to lose Bee-Bop. Not now. He clutched the robot to his chest.

"Just over-ridden the robot's circuits, temporarily. It will be fine in a few minutes," replied the computer.

"What do you want this time?" Whenever Pax was feeling sad or lonely, Alderman would chat with him. Pax wasn't sure if the computer did this to all the kids in the workhouses or whether he was being singled out for some unknown reason.

"I heard what was said in the Commandant's office earlier."

"Bully for you. You want a medal?" It was said the computer could listen to every conversation going on in London simultaneously.

"You don't have to accept this punishment."

Pax frowned in puzzlement. "Alderman, you may have the biggest brain in London, but even you can't disobey a direct order."

"You could apply to Scholastic Parliament, you know. Every child has that right, whatever their background. It's called Parliamentary Privilege."

Pax thought about the elite school, full of books and wonderful workshops. A pipedream. He scoffed. "Me? I'd never pass the exam."

"You have great potential."

"Great potential? I think your circuits have been infected."

"I assure you, I am completely devoid of any viruses or malware. You forget, Pax. I help run the seedling programme. I chose your genetic donors."

All the workhouse children were seedlings – born artificially from eggs fertilised in a laboratory.

"Then how come you've never suggested Parliamentary thingy before now? I've had plenty of other punishments."

"You were too young before. But there is a new school year starting soon. And you are now the perfect age to start at the senior school."

Pax thought about getting out of the workhouse three years early. It did sound tempting. But nobody else he knew had ever tried this escape route before. It seemed too good to be true. He narrowed his eyes. "There's got to be a catch."

Silence.

"Alderman?"

"If you fail the test, which you won't, you would be sent down the mines instead."

"The mines!" Pax shook his head. The mines were worse than ratting. Much worse. At least ratters always came back for a night's sleep. The mining crews had to stay down for days at a time. When they did emerge, blinking into the sun, there was no pong. Just the sound of coal dust rattling around lungs. If they came back at all. Pax thought about the twins and their accident for the second time that day. Each time, he felt like something inside him was malfunctioning, and he couldn't repair it.

"No thanks, Alderman. I'll take my chances in the sewers. At least I've still got my recycling duties to look forward to, every afternoon."

As others entered the dormitory, the light on Bee-Bop faded and Pax quickly hid the robot. It was nearly bedtime. Pax hurried to brush his teeth, as dozens of others jostled for position in the large, white-tiled communal bathroom. Everyone was rushing to be ready for bed before curfew.

The lights in the dormitory shut off abruptly just as Pax was heading back to his bed. In the gloom, he reached into his drawer and retrieved his treasured book of fairy tales. That and his atlas were the only mementos of the twins he had left.

He pulled the thin sheets over his head and reached under the pillow, extracting a wind-up torch. Another thing he had made from spare parts. He turned the handle a few times until the torch began to glow. He opened the book and found his place. Reading from the curled-up yellowed pages, Pax escaped from his troubles, for a while at least.

CHAPTER FOUR

Pax didn't think he'd been asleep for long when the alarm woke him. Rising groggily, he realised it was too early for the usual klaxon. This was the drone raid alert. Other heads popped up from their pillows. Soon everybody was scurrying towards the basement in their pyjamas, grumbling about the timing of this latest attack.

Most drone raids these days were an inconvenience rather than a threat, but protocols had to be obeyed. Pax had managed to grab a jumper as he joined the queue at the top of the basement stairs. Charlie helped count heads and found some blankets for the younger ones to use in the cool of the underground bomb shelter.

Pax looked around the familiar basement. A couple of buckets stank in the corner, serving as emergency toilets when the raids went on too long for young bladders. There was a tap for water and a cupboard stocked with hard, tasteless biscuits. No sign of the Commandant, as usual. Pax wondered if Hairy Hanson was up on the roof top, helping to spot the attackers but, somehow, he doubted it. More likely, the man had retreated to a bunker of luxury.

The huge wall-glass looming over the seats flickered to life. The anthem of New London blared out from hidden speakers, as the image of the familiar fluttering pennant filled the screen. Pax's nostrils flared at the thought of another infuriating propaganda speech. The Lord Mayor's red-cheeked face came into focus as the image of the flag faded.

"My fellow citizens. Once again, we find ourselves subject to an unprovoked attack from the aged empire outside our city walls. The Countryside Alliance may have wealth, but we have youth.

They may have land, but we have justice. We will never surrender!" Spittle collected on each side of the mayor's mouth as he worked himself up into a feverish tone. "The day is coming when we can throw open our gates and reclaim the whole country. Prepare yourselves. The time approaches!"

Computer-generated images of Defence League soldiers marching over England's green, rolling hills replaced the mayor's face. Stirring music played and Charlie stood up, saluting the screen. Charlie didn't like the mayor any more than Pax did, but he was fiercely loyal to New London.

Pax just rolled his eyes. "That's all we need. Why can't the Mayor and the King just get together and figure out their differences…"

"Peace? An end to the civil war? You've spent too long on top of the verti-farms with your head in the clouds," said Charlie.

Pax thought that sounded a lot better than being stuck down a sewer. But when the klaxon signalled the end of the raid, that was where he was headed. His first day of ratting duty.

[-]

It wasn't as bad as Pax thought it might be. It was worse. The stench of the sewers, even through the protection of a face mask, was enough to make Pax gag five times in the first hour. The sights turned his stomach. He was grateful that in the hurry to get ready after the drone raid, he'd not had time for breakfast.

It didn't help than none of the other members of his rat crew paid him any attention. They must have been through the same experience on their first rota down here. But instead of showing sympathy, they just plodded through their tasks as if the depressing atmosphere of the brick-lined sewers had sucked the life out of them.

Pax tried to imagine he was back on top of the verti-farms, looking at the sky and the birds but he couldn't sustain the illusion. For the next few hours, he picked at a gruesome blockage in the sewers with a pole that ended in a hook and spike. In the oppression of the tunnels, he felt as dark and dank as his surroundings.

When he got back, the workhouse had never seemed so bright and fresh. After a change of clothes and a thorough wash, Pax hurried along to the canteen. He was famished. Grabbing a tray of food, he looked for Charlie but couldn't see him anywhere. Remembering the older boy's advice about finding some new friends, Pax weighed up his options.

Giving up on his ratting crew, he sat down at a half-full table with seedlings he knew from the recycling lab. They wrinkled their noses at his presence and shifted along to keep as much distance as possible from him. The curse of a ratter. The conversation of the others continued as if Pax were not there.

"I hear two more drones got through this morning," said Thomas.

"Another two?!" replied Anne, a small girl with big eyes.

"Yeah. They flew in through an open window, snatched a baby and took it back beyond The Wall," continued Thomas.

"I hate those Pinchers," said another boy. *Pinchers* – the violent faction within the Countryside Alliance.

"Has anyone checked our windows?" asked Anne in a quavering voice.

"They're not big enough to take you, silly!" said Thomas. "Tell her, Pax."

Pleased to be invited to join the discuss, Pax smiled. "Oh, well, actually the Octo-blade 3000 is really cool. Very powerful. It could easily…" Pax paused, seeing the rising panic in Anne's face. "Oh, sorry. I mean, look. It couldn't get in here, I'm sure. No, you're definitely safe, Anne."

Thomas stared at Pax, open-mouthed. "Way to go, Pax."

Somebody put a consoling arm around Anne who was gulping for air.

Pax picked at his food, feeling very alone.

[-]

He was woken by a cough near his bed. Pax opened bleary eyes and looked at the Rota Clock – an old analogue 24-hour dial in the dorm, divided into three coloured segments. Still two hours before the red zone ended. Too early for the sun to creep through the windows, despite the thin curtains. He ached from yesterday's efforts in the sewers and their rank smell seemed to have seeped into his bedding overnight.

There was another cough from nearby and this time the person couldn't control it, wracking their lungs over and over. Pax turned to see a smudge-faced girl spit grey phlegm into a rag. She stuffed the rag back into her pocket when she saw Pax looking and instead held out a smashed-up head-torch.

"Charlie said you might be able to help."

Pax knuckled his eyes and swung his legs out of bed. "It's Clara, isn't it?" She had the bad luck of being on mining duty. That alone was worthy of sympathy. But as her chin began to wobble, it was clear something was especially wrong today. "What happened?"

Tears rolled down her cheeks, carving paths through the grime on her face.

"We was at the end of our shift, waiting by the surface lifts when a blummin' rat ran across my foot." The girl dropped her gaze to the floor and picked at her lips. "I know we should be used to them by now. But this one woz really big. And it had pink eyes. Pink! I jumped and banged me head."

"Let me see." Pax took the torch from Clara and turned it over in his hands, assessing the damage. He reached into his bedside drawer, lifted up the false bottom and pulled out a small set of tools. He began to take apart the broken light.

"Can you fix it? Hairy Hanson will have me on short rations if he finds out."

"Well, the battery and contacts seem fine," he replied. "But you'll need to replace the bulb and find a new plexi-cover."

"How am I supposed to get those flippin' things before 8 o' clock inspection?" Clara leant forward and began to sob, wrapping arms across her stomach. "Sorry, Pax. Didn't mean to snap. I'm starved that's all."

A few hours in the recycling lab, and Pax was sure he could steal the parts for her. But not at this time in the morning. He looked at Clara. He knew all too well that feeling of dizziness when hunger gnawed at your stomach, threatening to topple you at the slightest breeze.

Pax sighed and rubbed at the metallic dots on the back of his head. He reached under the pillow for his home-made torch. He took it apart and used the bulb to replace Clara's broken one. He compared the plexi-covers of the two torches; not quite the same. After a few minutes of cutting, snipping and smoothing, his cover fitted the head-torch and it was as good as new.

"Oh, thank you, Pax!" Clara was about to throw her arms around him when he held out a hand.

"That's alright. Just don't cover me with coal dust, OK?"

Clara looked down at her filthy overalls and grinned. "I don't care what the others say about ya. You're totally urbane!" The girl turned and ran off to the showers.

Pax got back into bed and lay there, trying to figure out when he might get replacement parts for his own torch. And trying not to think about another morning spent down in the sewers.

CHAPTER FIVE

Pax couldn't get back to sleep, so he got dressed and wandered the corridors of the workhouse, still quiet with the red-shift teams not due back for another hour or so. Alderman's holographic head appeared ahead of him, floating in the air. Pax stopped in his tracks.

"Have you thought some more about Parliamentary Privilege?"

Not this again! Pax grunted and kept walking, passing straight through the hologram. Alderman's head re-appeared a little further down the corridor.

"What you did for Clara, Pax, that was very kind. Why did you help her?"

"I like fixing things, OK? Stop bugging me."

"You could become an Engineer, you know, if you graduated from Scholastic Parliament."

Pax stopped and stared at the floating head. "The Guild of Engineers…" He'd never before dared dream of a life like that.

"You would have your own workshop in time."

The first ray of sunlight peeped through a window, spreading warmth across Pax's face. He closed his eyes and smiled, imagining himself in charge of a workshop. No, impossible. He shook his head and frowned. "Why do you even care?"

"My job is to maximise the welfare of all the citizens of New London. I do not like to see potential like yours wasted."

"I'd never keep up with the other kids – they've had proper educations. They've got real parents. The right up-bringing to succeed."

"None of that matters, Pax. It is what is inside that counts. But you must declare soon. Term starts in less than a week."

Pax shook his head. "I'm not risking those mines. Ratting is grim, but I still have recycling duties to look forward to every afternoon. Now leave me be."

Alderman's head disappeared. Pax made his way to the canteen for an early breakfast, trying to ignore the seed of hope the super-computer had planted in his mind. An Engineer...

[-]

Two days later, when Pax got back from another miserable shift down in the sewers, he found a parcel waiting for him on his bed with a note attached. He looked around the dormitory. Nobody ever got post. His legs jigged up and down in nervous excitement as he sat to read the note.

Pax. I got the call up for the D.F. earlier than expected. Some sort of recruitment drive. I'm off to The Wall! Sorry I missed you, Charlie

Pax drew in a shuddering breath and screwed up the piece of paper. Just before he threw it into a bin, he noticed a second part to the message on the back.

PS Thought you might like these, I'll get a new pair on the Wall

He unwrapped the parcel, his curiosity piqued. It was Charlie's night-vision goggles. As one of the oldest boys in the workhouse, his extra responsibilities during drone raids included being a spotter on the roof. Such a wonderful gift. Pax couldn't wait to try them on later that evening. But he would rather have Charlie still around. With a rueful smile, he went to get some lunch.

Pax collected his food and scanned the tables. His heart sank as he realised there was no point in looking for Charlie. His ratting crew were still giving him the cold-shoulder for some reason. He spotted Thomas, Anne and the rest of his recycling group, but as he headed towards them, they subtly shifted on their benches, ensuring there was no gap left at their table.

Finally, Pax saw a space next to Ginger and sat down.

She sniffed the air, but didn't turn her back or move away. "Sewers treating you well?"

Pax grunted. "Sorry. Can't seem to shift the smell, no matter how much I scrub. Do you want me to sit somewhere else?"

"Nah, you're alright. Pax."

He smiled with relief. He wondered if it was worth the pain of starting up a new friendship. None of his friends ever seemed to stick around. They just stole a piece of your heart, and never gave it back. But it was, at least, nice to have somebody to talk to at meal times. His relief was punctured by the appearance of Commandant Hanson in the canteen.

Everybody snapped to attention, the room filled with the noise of twenty benches scraping back.

The Commandant's voice boomed out. "New London is no place for losers."

"We will win!" shouted the room in unison as chests were thumped and the victory sign made. The Commandant gestured for everyone to sit down.

"It has come to my attention," he said, "that 44G13 has rather foolishly caught bronchitis. And even worse, she appears to have given it to 43B12. The doctor insists they both stay in bed for a few days. Bah! Which means there is a gap in the farming roster. I need two volunteers for extra duties."

Pax almost lifted from the bench as he stretched his hand towards the ceiling his heartbeat skipping at the thought of peace and joy on the verti-farms. Hanson stared straight past Pax and looked across the sea of faces.

"Anybody else?"

"But sir, I'm the most experienced farmer here," said Pax, his eyebrows furrowed in frustration.

"Bah! I didn't ask for a discussion 45B1, I asked for volunteers. Now then, let's see. You'll get double helpings at supper."

As soon as the Commandant said this, a host of other hands were raised. He pointed to a boy and a girl on the far side of the room. "You two, report to the hover bay, immediately." Then he turned to look at Pax again. "As for you, I think an extra shift in the sewers might teach you some manners."

Pax couldn't believe it. "But you can't…"

"Let's make it a week of double shifts in the sewers. I'm sure the recycling lab can do without you for a while."

"That's not fair!" Pax shouted, unable to control his emotions.

"A month," said the Commandant with a lop-sided grin.

Pax's knuckles turned white as his hands curled into tight fists. He tried to keep his mouth shut, drawing in deep breaths through his nose as anger threatened to boil his blood. Taking away his recycling duties, the only thing he liked doing was not just unfair, it was cruel. He couldn't stand this treatment anymore. "No," he whispered.

Hanson's bushy eyebrows lifted like a pair of startled caterpillars. "I beg your pardon?"

"I said no." Louder now, more determined. He stared at the Commandant, knowing what he had to do. The canteen fell into silence as everybody turned to watch the confrontation.

Hanson stepped closer to Pax, leaning over him. "It wasn't a suggestion, boy. Do you really want to refuse my order?"

Pax didn't move but just stared up at the man.

"Do you want me to get The Arm involved?"

Pax swallowed hard. "I claim Parliamentary Privilege."

The rest of the room gasped. Hanson's fierce face crumbled for a moment, replaced by a look of doubt. He looked around the room and quickly regained his fierce demeanour.

"Very well. I shall enjoy watching you fail. And end up down the mines." The Commandant turned to exit. He glanced around the room one more time. "What are you miserable specimens looking at! Finish your food and get back to work! Bah!"

As soon as he had left, excited conversations erupted across the room. Had anyone ever stood up to Hairy Hanson before? None that Pax could remember.

Ginger leant towards him with a grin. "Wow, didn't see that coming. The sewers finally got to you, did they?" She used her fork to jab at a grey lump on Pax's plate.

"He hates me," replied Pax.

"He hates us all. But I think he's worried."

"Worried about what?"

"Doesn't want you to pass the test."

"What difference is it to him?" asked Pax. "Pass or fail, I'm out of his hair. Probably fail."

"Yeah, but if you pass…" She plucked some more food from Pax's plate, much to his annoyance. "…you could come back one day as his boss. Imagine that!"

[-]

Pax sat in front of a dusty, 25-year-old computer terminal in the middle of a small room. *Dithering diodes!* He was surprised it still worked, knowing the model and spec quite well from his time in the recycling labs. Obviously, the workhouse made no effort to keep the test equipment up to date.

A set of drawers, a bin and a spare chair had been shoved untidily into a corner. The white walls were bare and windowless. The only way in or out of the room was a plain door, next to which stood Miss Scrubs, her arms folded.

Pax stared at the words on the screen.

Scholastic Parliament Entrance Exam. 60 marks available

"You will have one hour to answer as many questions as possible," said Miss Scrubs as she placed a timer on the desk next to Pax. Leaning next to his ear, she whispered good luck before straightening up again. "Your time starts now."

Pax watched the numbers on the timer begin to count back from 60:00, took a deep breath and pressed enter on the grimy keyboard. He stared at the first multiple-choice question. Cold sweat broke out on his forehead as he realised he didn't have a clue who was Karl Marx. Alderman had got it all wrong. Pax didn't stand a chance of passing the test. He wondered what madness had overcome him in the canteen earlier, regretting his rash boldness. Surely he was headed for the mines.

Pax plumped for one of the options, drawing a 'humph' from Miss Scrubs, and moved on to question two, about the first British civil war. He thought he knew the answer to this question, selected a button and looked at question three. Yes! A question on IT equipment. He didn't even have to think about this one.

He became so engrossed in the exam, he barely noticed Miss Scrubs slip away. He had reached question eighteen, feeling a bit more confident about his chances of success, when the room was plunged into darkness. A moment later, the computer terminal screen went blank. The only source of light remaining was the green glow of the figures on the timer.

Sizzling circuits!

Pax stabbed at some buttons on the keyboard as panic gripped his chest. Nothing happened. He banged the side of the terminal's screen. Again nothing. He got up, fumbled his way to the door and tried the handle. Locked. His heart squeezed tight as he thumped on the door. No response.

When he glanced up at a red dot in the corner of the ceiling, he noticed the security camera. It was probably just his imagination but it seemed to be grinning at him. He thought about Ginger's warning. *Hanson doesn't want you to pass…*

The timer counted down towards his destiny.

CHAPTER SIX

T he timer showed 27 minutes, 56 seconds left. Pax shoved his hands in his pockets, wishing he'd never listened to Alderman's crazy idea. Hairy Hanson was going to be so smug when Pax failed.

His fingers brushed against two items and after a moment he realised what he had in his pockets. The LED lights and the battery he'd filched from the recycling lab a few days ago. He connected them up and used the light to search around the room. In the drawers he found a pair of scissors, some paperclips, a pen, a pad and a rubber.

An idea began to form. He nodded to himself.

Rattling resistors! I'm not giving Hairy Hanson the satisfaction.

He unwrapped the length of flex he used for a belt and pulled the desk across the room until it was under the security camera. Standing on the desk, he used the scissors to remove the plastic casing from the camera. He shoved a paperclip into the rubber and used it as a make-shift screwdriver to avoid getting electrocuted. He attached the wire in the flex to the camera's power source. Its tiny red light showed the camera still had juice.

Pax jumped down from the desk and ran his flex to the computer terminal. After a bit more fiddling, he connected the computer up to the camera's power source. He crossed his fingers and tried the on button. The computer whirred into life. He breathed deeply, glancing up at the camera with a grin.

As the computer booted up, Pax heard footsteps in the corridor outside. If this power cut was deliberate, who knew what else they might try to stop him taking the test. He jumped up and rammed the spare chair under the door handle just as it began to turn. Somebody thumped on the door.

"Open up, Pax!" shouted Miss Scrubs from outside.

Pax ignored her and, on the computer screen, navigated his way back to the Scholastic Parliament Entrance Exam website. He groaned when he realised his progress had not been saved. His fingers were a blur as he hurried to re-enter his details and started the exam back at question one.

He glanced across at the timer. 21 minutes, 12 seconds.

He rattled through the first eighteen questions, desperately trying to remember the answers he'd already chosen. He finally got to a new question with nineteen minutes to go. He had no idea how many he would need to get right to pass the exam. But surely he didn't have time?

He read the questions as quickly as possible, choosing an option each time as soon as he had a vague inkling of an answer. There was no time to ponder, weighing up options. Miss Scrubs stopped pounding on the door at last.

Question thirty. Ten minutes to go. A section on engineering. Pax flew through that. Question forty. Five minutes to go. Verbal reasoning. Complicated statements and logic trails to follow. He could do them but not at speed. And the banging on the door had resumed, disturbing his concentration.

Geography for the last ten questions. One minute to go. Pax loved maps. He never got to travel but, in his imagination, when he stared at a map he could be anywhere in the world. He raced through half of the section and then the timer beeped. Pax removed the chair jamming the door shut and let in Miss Scrubs.

She wasn't alone. Commandant Hanson glared down at Pax, his cheeks flushed red, his chest heaving.

Pax stepped back. "Sorry about the mess, sir. There seems to have been a completely unexplained power cut in the room, halfway through my test."

"You won't be able to take the test again."

"No sir."

The Commandant's look of fury morphed into a smile. "Looks like you'll be heading down the mines after all."

"Well, it was a bit of a rush, but I managed most of the test despite the set-back. So, I guess it depends on whether I got enough right, won't it? Sir."

Pax reached across to the computer terminal and swivelled the monitor towards Commandant Hanson. He pressed a key and an egg-timer appeared next to the word 'Evaluating.' Pax gulped and crossed his fingers.

Please not the mines. I want to be an Engineer. Please not the mines.

A moment later the computer pinged and the message changed to 'Congratulations Candidate 45B1, you have passed.'

"Yes!" Pax punched the air as a wave of euphoria washed over him.

Commandant Hanson barged Pax out of the way and yanked the makeshift wires out of the back of the computer. The screen went blank once again.

He jabbed a finger at Pax. "You did not pass the test!" And then turned to Miss Scrubs. "And you did not see that result!"

"But... but... you can't do this!" shouted Pax as the heady bubbles of elation quickly turned into a seething cauldron of lava inside him.

"And who is going to stop me? Scrubs, take him back to the dorms while he awaits his assignment down in the mines."

Miss Scrubs held out an arm, a sad face on her look. "Come on, Pax."

[-]

Pax lay miserably on his bed, staring glassy-eyed up at the ceiling. Bee-Bop was playing a tune, moving in and out of the legs of the bed. Ginger appeared. She reached for the little robot, found the off-switch and put it back in Pax's drawer.

"You tried to warn me," he said at last.

"You need to get up, Pax," she replied.

"What's the point?"

"You have a visitor." Ginger had a strange smirk on her face.

Pax heaved himself up, despite the lump of lead sitting heavy in his stomach. He thought Ginger might have shown a bit more sympathy, not found it funny. "The mining supervisor, I suppose?"

Ginger shook her head and winked, retreating from his bed. As she did so, Pax caught sight of a Beefeater approaching in full black-and-red-striped uniform. The man looked like a hideous ogre from the book of fairy tales. Pax gulped, wondering if he would even make it to the mines alive. He knew that the Beefeaters formed the personal guard for the mayor but he had only ever seen one on a wall-glass before today.

"Come with me," said the walking mountain.

Pax bit his nails, wondering what new punishment awaited him now.

The Beefeater escorted Pax back to Hairy Hanson's office. But that's not who was waiting for him. Despite the glaring sun once again forcing Pax to squint, there was no mistaking the figure sitting behind the desk. Silas Letherington, the Lord Mayor himself. Not on a wall glass. In the flesh, here in Workhouse Five!

"Ahh, welcome young man."

Pax was too stunned to move. After a moment he remembered to thump his fist against his chest and performed the salute.

The mayor nodded to acknowledge the salute and gestured towards the chair. "No need for ceremony. Come in, sit down."

This was absurd. Pax's attempt to join Scholastic Parliament had just ended in disaster and here he was being offered a seat by New London's longest-serving leader. Pax reached for the chair and collapsed into it, unable to control his muscles properly. Terror, excitement, curiosity all fought for priority in his mind.

"Congratulations 45B1, or should I say, Pax."

Pax shook his head trying to figure out what was going on. "Err, for what your Lordship?"

"For passing the entrance exam."

Pax's brain was so scrambled in the presence of the mayor it was as if his thoughts were wading through treacle. "But I thought... the computer crashed. Didn't it?"

33

The mayor shook his head. "Not before it had sent the results through to our central monitoring station. We can hardly leave the results to be collected by some lowly official like Hanson. All the workhouse leaders try to keep hold of their best workers. Some try harder than others. But it didn't stop you, did it?"

Pax gripped the arms of his chair, scarcely able to believe what he was hearing. Did this mean… A bubble of happiness was rising up his throat, trapping all the questions Pax was desperate to ask.

The mayor continued. "We reviewed the security footage. Most ingenious, young man. And one of the highest marks we've ever seen for this exam."

Pax stared at the mayor, open-mouthed, tears beginning to form.

"Alderman always said the seedling programme would produce results one day. Thought I'd come and see if he was right after all. You're not quite the first seedling to pass the test but certainly the brightest, judging from these results. Difficult to believe those answers came from the slack-jawed boy I see before me."

Pax wiped at his eyes. "Sorry, your Lordship. It's a bit of a shock, that's all. Sir, why did you choose Westminster Palace as the site of the school?"

"It seemed a shame to waste the building after we'd got rid of all those squabbling politicians. And what better way to show our commitment to youth than by putting our brightest at the heart of New London. Well, no need to dawdle. Go and gather your things. Term starts tomorrow. Don't want to be late on your first day." The mayor waved a hand towards the exit.

Pax stood up and bowed. "Thank you, your Lordship."

"We'll certainly be keeping an eye on you, 45B1."

As Pax left the room, he heard the mayor talking to the Beefeater. "Make sure the Commandant understands the full extent of my displeasure."

Pax smiled and hurried back to the dormitory.

Hah, serves Hairy Hanson right!

He packed his bag. He wrapped Bee-Bop in his pyjamas. Some spare underwear. His toolkit and Charlie's old night-vision goggles. His broken head torch and his tattered old books. A

34

toothbrush and a few pieces of recycled tech he hadn't yet found a use for. He hoped there would be a new boiler suit waiting for him. He didn't want the smell of ratting duty to follow him to his new school.

He checked under his bed and had one last look in his drawers.

"In a hurry to leave?" said Ginger.

Pax turned in surprise. He found it hard to look her in the eye. "News travels fast, I guess. Sorry."

"Don't apologise. Most of us would give our left arm to be going where you are."

"There must be loads of mice in a big, old building like that. I'll catch some and send them over."

"No, you won't," she replied with a rueful smile.

Pax opened his mouth to protest but she just shook her head.

"Just do me a favour, yeah? Show them wombats that us seedlings are just as good as them. Alright?"

Pax nodded and picked up his bag with a shaking hand. Workhouse five was all he'd ever known. Even though he hated the place, suddenly he felt reluctant to leave. He looked around the room one last time and swallowed down his fears. What had the mayor said – one of the best marks ever? Pax shouldered his bag and stood tall. It was time.

Scholastic Parliament, here I come.

PART TWO

THE PALACE

CHAPTER SEVEN

From the side of the road, Pax paused to admire Westminster Palace – the home of Scholastic Parliament – as the two wings and many towers stretched out. Honey-coloured ribs of Gothic stonework glowed in the September sunshine. Sounds of boats and the smell of mudbanks hinted at the Thames on the far side of the building. Pax followed the other pupils in through St Sephen's porch, leaving his old life behind.

At the school's heart, Pax stood on the rich, mosaic floor of the tall octagonal Central Lobby. The young ones starting junior school today had already filed off to his left. Pax wondered if they'd needed to sit an exam or if their potential had been identified some other way. Most started at the younger age, but each year a few pupils like Pax were allowed to join at the start of senior phase, around their twelfth birthday.

He was wearing a grey boiler suit that identified him as a member of the Party of Judges. It had been a pleasant surprise to find overalls that actually fitted. Somehow, the school had known his measurements and the uniform had been waiting for him.

He looked around the chamber at the different coloured boiler suits and tried to remember what his greeting pack had said about the other three parties to which pupils were assigned. Loyals were in red, Peers in green and blue for Chancellors.

Wherever he looked he saw badges sewn onto the breast pocket with a simple circle as its emblem, the same as his. This meant everybody here was a first-year senior. They had been told to wait here until called for the first assembly of term. The atmosphere was so alien to Pax, from the beauty of the building to the proud bearing of the other pupils. He'd never been surrounded by so many strangers in his life.

He stared up at the decorative golden ceiling that seemed to radiate warmth and comfort, but he could feel neither. Nervous energy thrummed along his limbs. Hemmed in by the others, he shifted his weight from foot to foot, feeling isolated despite the crowd. Everyone else was already in conversation with their neighbour.

"Not seen you around, squirt."

Pax turned to the voice and looked up into a pale face framed with jet-black, straight hair. He was wearing red for Loyal. Red for rude.

"My name's Pax, not squirt."

"Well, Pax, a little droney told me you got top marks in the entrance exam. A Pinhead like you? Must have cheated, I reckon." He turned to the other pupils in red who were watching this conversation. They nodded their agreement.

Pax's hand went to rub the metallic dots on the back of his head. *Pinhead.*

"Don't worry," continued the other boy. "We know just what to do with cheats, around here. And squirts who don't know their place." He stepped a little closer. "I'm Zachariah, by the way."

He held out his hand. Pax, confused at the welcome, went to shake hands but regretted it immediately. Zachariah's grip was vice-like. As his fingers were crushed, Pax tried not to cry out but a little whimper escaped from his pursed lips. There were titters of laughter from the people watching.

A teacher arrived to call them into assembly and the crowd surged forwards. Pax hung back trying to put as much distance as possible between himself and the gang of red Loyals. His first encounter had just confirmed his worst fears. Nobody here was going to welcome an outsider like him. A girl with long blonde hair, in a grey boiler suit, approached.

"Pax, was it? Alright? I see you've met Zachariah Thomson," she said with a Welsh accent. "He was such a big-head in junior school. Always showing off, putting others down. Ignore him."

Pax looked at the smiling girl, grateful for a kind word at last. "Right," he replied, his senses too over-loaded to say any more.

"I'm Megan, by the way. Looks like we're in the same Party. Come on, don't want to be late for Miss Adams on day one. Don't say much, do you?"

Assembly was held in a grand room filled with rows of red leather benches. The stained-glass windows and gold-leaf detail on the furnishings glistened in the bright, September afternoon sunshine, as if everything were shiny and new. Pupils filed through the iron gates at the entrance and arranged themselves on the tiered rows of seats. Friends shuffled along to sit next to each other, accompanied by the sound of bottoms squeaking on the leather.

Pax wanted to go and sit in one of the empty sections, but he noticed that the four different Parties had already grouped themselves. The clump of grey boiler suits was on his left, in the back two rows. He followed Megan and joined the other Judges. A silence quickly fell on the room as the Headmistress, Miss Adams, stood to address everybody from her throne-like seat at the head of the chamber. She wore a pale blue dress that matched her eyes and perched slim reading glasses on the end of her nose.

"Order, order! Settle down." Her voice carried across the huge room with ease. "Thank you. Welcome to the start of a new Scholastic year, especially to those pupils joining us for the first time. I am sure that with hard work, dedication and the will to win, you'll fit in just fine here. The Parliamentary Polls begin at once, of course. No doubt the Loyals are going to enjoy their extra privileges after last year's victory. But remember, failure will not be tolerated. I'm sure the Judges wish they had tried a little harder last year."

Pax gulped. It looked like he'd ended up in the worst party. Miss Adams continued with a gesture to a group of students at the back of the room. "These second-years will show you to your accommodation, where you will unpack as quickly and quietly as possible. You will then follow the signs to the canteen and after supper, you will retire to your bedrooms for an early night. Tomorrow, your time at Scholastic Parliament will begin in earnest and you will need all the rest you can get." She peered over her glasses and looked around the room. Was it Pax's imagination, or did she stare straight at him for a moment longer than necessary?

[-]

The wood-panelled Judges' common room was dominated by a large fireplace and several sofas. Above the fireplace was the Judges' emblem – a grey boulder – and around the edges of the room were tables and chairs.

Sukhwinder, the second-year boy who had shown them the way, had the same grey boiler suit as the other Judges, but his badge had a diagonal cross instead of a circle. He told everybody the code for the keypad on the door into the common room. "It changes every term. And keep it secret, remember. No other Parties are allowed in here."

Pax tried to memorise the number. 45862. 4-5-8-6-2. He saw somebody scribbling the code on the back of their hand. Sukhwinder then assigned rooms to everyone, in alphabetical order, ending with Wang, Chen and Williams, Megan.

"Right, is that everybody?"

Pax gulped, wondering if he'd missed something. He slowly raised his hand.

"Oh, err, you must be the seedling." Sukhwinder consulted his digi-pad. "45B1, isn't it? Hmm."

"Is there a problem?" asked Pax, blushing as all eyes turned to him.

"It's just there are lots of things done alphabetically here. And 45B1 is going to mess things up a bit. Do you go before A, or after Z?"

Surrounded by Wombats – people born naturally – Pax had hoped his differences to everyone else wouldn't be quite so obvious on the first day. He wasn't sure what to say. He just wanted the ground to swallow him up.

"Well?" continued Sukhwinder.

"Why don't we give him a surname?" suggested Megan. "Hmm, let's think. Four-Bee. How does Forby sound, Pax?"

Pax blinked. A surname. It was the nicest present he'd ever received. "Pax Forby... that would be lovely." He smiled at Megan.

41

"Right, Forby, you're rooming with Samuel Banton," said Sukhwinder.

Pax's new roommate was nearly as tall as Zachariah, but that's where the similarities ended. Samuel's black hair was curled and his hands were soft when they shook in greeting. They were directed up three flights of stairs to a room with a sloped ceiling and two beds pushed up against opposite walls. A small window looked out over the roof, towards Westminster's famous clock tower. It didn't take long for Pax to unpack his things. He was pleased to find a spare, grey boiler suit and some PE kit laid out on his bed.

Samuel still hadn't said much apart from hello. Maybe he was just following Miss Adams' instructions for quiet. But Pax was full of questions. "This Parliamentary Poll, how does it work?"

Samuel carried on unpacking, keeping his back to Pax as he spoke. "Every pupil gains or loses points for their Party throughout the year, depending on good or bad behaviour, high or low scores in tests. And there are special events through the year that are worth bonuses points. At the end of the year, the Party with the most points, wins. I thought everybody knew that."

Pax shrugged. "Scholastic Parliament is like another world to workhouse kids. What does winning the Poll mean?"

Samuel stopped unpacking and turned to face Pax. "The third years in the winning party, who are graduating, get the first pick of jobs available in New London. The first and second years, who are staying on, get special privileges for their next year at school."

"Sounds nice. And the losers?"

"The party what comes last gets punished, course. New London is no place for losers 'n' all that. The third years graduating well, they might not get a job at all. The other years have workhouse duties all summer."

That doesn't sound so bad, thought Pax.

"And two people get expelled."

Pax felt his mouth run dry. If the Judges came last again, he might end up back with Hairy Hanson. And he'd never become an Engineer. "How do they choose which pupils?"

"Random pick. It's called the Draft," said Samuel with a shrug. He stared at Pax. "What was the workhouse like?"

Pax didn't know how to answer. What did he have to compare it against? "It was OK, I suppose. I mean, as long as you stayed away from the sewers and the mines."

Samuel shot him a look of pain as Pax said that last word, then fell silent. Pax wasn't sure what he'd said wrong but, before he could ask, an electronic chime rang out twice from a speaker in the ceiling.

"That'll be supper," said Samuel. "Come on, let's eat."

The two boys made their way out of the common room. The building was a warren of stone passageways, classrooms and courtyards overlooked by lead windows in the surrounding corridors. Grand, wide staircases or winding steps tucked away in the corner of corridors connected several different floor levels. Pax revelled in the wide, airy spaces while Samuel pointed out interesting features, including a supposedly haunted cupboard called The Caretaker's Coffin.

Pax didn't believe in ghosts but he couldn't wait to get hold of a map of the building. He tried to memorise the route as Samuel led the way, eventually arriving at the canteen. The large rectangular room had a high ceiling, a serving hatch in one corner and several rows of long, thin tables with wooden benches. At first, Pax thought he would be too nervous to eat, meeting all these new faces. But after a busy day and with the smell of butter and brine tantalising his tastebuds, he found his appetite. They queued up for a bowl of steaming broth and a roll of bread.

"Oh, not whelk soup!" cried Samuel.

Pax knew the Thames was an important source of food these days, along with the verti-farms, but the workhouse canteen never had access to seafood. His mouth was salivating. "You should try workhouse gruel sometime."

Samuel tutted and headed towards the far end of the room. Walking past all the other tables, Pax could tell from the colours of the boiler suits they were divided by Parties. Loyals nearest the serving hatch, Judges furthest away, Peers and Chancellors in between. He wondered if this reflected last year's Parliamentary Poll result. Not that a few extra steps bothered him.

They sat at a table with other first-year Judges and Pax was pleased to see a space next to Megan. She looked up and smiled. Finally, Pax felt his shoulder muscles relax. Maybe Scholastic Parliament wasn't going to be so scary after all.

CHAPTER EIGHT

Pax and Samuel made their way down for breakfast. The canteen buzzed with excitement as Pax caught snippets of conversations.

"You went to the Manchester Metropolis! What was that like?"

"This is going to be Chancellors' year, I just know it."

"Is Miss Adams ever going to retire?"

Zachariah was just getting up from his table as Pax walked past with his tray of food. The larger boy bumped into him, making Pax's glass of juice slop over the tray.

"Oops, didn't see you there, squirt."

Pax hurried past, catching up to Samuel who hadn't seen the incident. As Pax sat down with the other first years, Megan looked at him. "He really doesn't like you, does he?"

"Who, Zachariah?" He shrugged. There'd been plenty of worse bullies back in the workhouse. "I can live with that."

"You have to stand up to people like that, Pax, or they'll just walk all over you. By the way, have you two decided what you're gonna do for the talent show yet?"

Pax's heart skipped a beat. "The... the what?"

Megan tutted. "You know, the *talent* show. First years have to come up with some sort of performance every year in front of the whole school. An initiation ritual, if you like. Toughen us up."

"Especially if you come last," said Samuel, taking a bite from his toast.

Pax gulped at the thought of standing up on stage. He'd lost his appetite despite the delicious butter oozing over the warm toast. "It's a competition?"

"Of course it is, silly," said Megan. "Points for the winner and the runner-up, minus points for whoever comes last. The whole school gets to vote. What you lot going to do, anyways?"

"Probably sing summit," replied Samuel.

"Ballet," said a girl called Briony.

Chen chopped the air with her hand. "Karate display."

"Tidy. I reckon I'll do a solo on my guitar," replied Megan.

They all turned to look at Pax, who was still staring at Briony.

"What do you like doing, Pax?" asked Samuel.

"What, me? Err… not being on stage."

Briony giggled.

The canteen fell silent as Miss Adams appeared in the doorway. Her long blue dress hid her feet. Pax could barely even see her legs move, as if the Headmistress was floating towards their table. He picked at his food, trying to avoid her gaze.

"Good morning, 45B1. Or should I say, Forby. How was your first night, here?"

His skin flushed hot and cold. It felt weird hearing his new surname. But why had she picked him out for a chat?

"Well? Pincher took your tongue?"

"Err, yes, fine thank you, Miss Adams. The others have been very kind, helping me settle. Explaining things." He looked around the table and flashed a nervous smile at the others.

"Good, good. It's been a while since we had a seedling join us. Glad to have you on board. You'll find lessons very hard at first. Having missed junior school, there will be a lot of catching up to do. But don't expect any special treatment."

"No, Miss."

"You'll need one of these." She handed him a brand-new wrist tab.

Pax gasped. It was so shiny. He'd seen lots before in the recycling lab, but they always had a cracked screen or the back had broken open. This one was perfect and now it was his. "Th… thanks."

"Carry on, then." And with that, she swept out of the room.

Pax began to play with the screen as he strapped it to his wrist. His fingers were shaking with excitement as Samuel showed him how to set up his Scholastic Parliament account and load the timetable app and Hansard – the social media chatline for pupils. He selected a username: SPF. Seedling Pax Forby.

"Come on," said Megan. "Don't want to be late for our first lesson."

Pax glanced at his wrist tab. Maths. He smiled as the tiny display showed the best route through the building to the West corridor, first floor, room C.

[-]

When they got to the correct room, Zachariah and all his friends had already occupied all the desks in the far corner of the class. A sea of red boiler suits. Pax chose a seat as far away as possible and stared open-mouthed at his new robotic teacher, wheeling about the room on a round base. At the end of a curved metal neck, the droid had a large screen that showed a simple emoji-type face. Two little speakers above his screen stuck up like animal's ears. He looked like a giant knight from an old-fashioned chess board.

"I am Sir Tristram," he announced.

"That's one of King Arthur's knights," Pax whispered to Samuel.

Samuel nodded. "The recharging station for all the robot teachers is a big circular device, so they are known as the Knights of the Round Table."

Pax smiled, remembering his book of myths. "Cool."

Because this was their very first lesson at senior school, Sir Tristram gave out a hinged circular band of steel to each pupil. "These are your new torcs. Put them around your neck, and use the button on the right to switch them on."

Pax watched Megan as she followed the teacher's instructions. Everybody else did the same and their torcs began to glow. Pax struggled into his. It felt heavy around his neck. Fumbling for the button, he turned it on and blinked in amazement. Shimmering in the air just in front of his face was a Heads-Up Display full of information and options. He could still see the classroom beyond, but only if he forced his eyes to focus in the distance. Instructions on how to use a special pen to take virtual notes appeared in his display.

Pax marvelled at the technology available to pupils here, wondering if the torcs or even the teachers had been made from parts he'd recycled back in the workshop. Clearly there wasn't a shortage of IT equipment for some people in New London. As the lesson began, Pax saw what Sir Tristram was saying appear in the main window of his HUD. When the teacher wrote on the main board at the front of the classroom, it appeared on Pax's screen too.

Back in the workhouse, Pax had always learnt by reading books after his duties were over for the day, going at his own pace, chatting with Alderman when he was alone. But now he was having to concentrate. The new technology was amazing, but the information came at him in rapid-fire waves.

Pax was determined to prove that a seedling could be as good as a wombat. He tried to take as many notes as possible. When he struggled to follow a section on trigonometry, he put up his hand. "Sir, what's a high-pot-amuse?"

There were sniggers from the Loyals as Sir Tristram wheeled towards Pax's desk. The teacher's emoji face was straight lipped. It blinked at him. "Hypotenuse, Forby. It's the long side of a right-angle triangle. You should know this already. It's very basic trigonometry."

"Yes, sir," said Pax, his cheeks flushing red. "Sorry."

"Remember, class," continued Sir Tristram, "if you get stuck during homework, your torcs have a built-in chatbot function."

"You mean we can talk to our torcs, sir?" said a boy from Chancellors.

"Yes, very good, Patel. This function will be locked out of use during tests and exams, of course."

Pax didn't ask any more questions. When the bell sounded, his HUD flashed *End of Lesson* in red then shut down. As the others scurried out of the room, Pax waited to ask Sir Tristram for some extra homework. If he was going to be an engineer, he couldn't afford to fail at maths. It was clear he had a lot of catching up to do, just like Miss Adams had warned him. The thought nibbled away at his fragile confidence, like beavers gnawing on a tree trunk.

Outside in the corridor, Pax saw that the others hadn't bothered waiting for him. He wrapped his arms around himself. This huge, ancient building suddenly felt very big and very cold.

CHAPTER NINE

Pax used his wrist tab to check on the next lesson. Geography with Sir Gawain. East corridor, second floor, room B. He rushed towards the stairs.

"Forby! What do you think you're doing?" It was one of the human teachers – Mrs Bowie, the music and drama teacher. She had big hoop earrings and wavy brown hair.

Pax froze, mid-corridor, looking around as other pupils filed around him. "M'am?"

"You're on the wrong side of the corridor, boy. Can't you see the line?"

Pax looked down at his feet and spotted a faint strip down the middle of the corridor. He realised all the pupils coming towards him were on the right side of the line, and those walking away from him were on the left. "Sorry, I didn't realise."

"Ignorance is no excuse. Alderman, deduct one point from the Judges."

The familiar voice of London's super-computer blurted out of a ceiling speaker somewhere above Pax's head "Acknowledged."

As Alderman said this, Pax felt a jolt of electricity pulse from his torc into his spine. "Ouch! My torc just zapped me."

"Of course it did, Forby," said Mrs Bowie. "Breaking the rules is a serious offence. Now hurry along to your next lesson. And stay on the left!"

Pax pulled at his torc, trying to take it off, but the hinge was locked in place. His breathing quickened as he realised this learning device was also an implement of discipline. His skin prickled under the weight of the metal noose but there was no way to relieve the itch.

He tried to distract himself by focusing on the next lesson. At least the Loyals were on a different timetable for this lesson. The directions on the wrist tab told him to cross the building at ground level and then go up some stairs near the Peers' party common room. He managed to stay on the correct side of the lines in the corridor. On the ground floor, he spotted some first-year Loyals starting to file into a class room for their second lesson of the day.

Pax didn't want to bump into Zachariah again, so he ducked into a dark side passage, waiting for the corridor to empty. But as he hid, he heard a familiar voice. The very person he was trying to avoid.

"Yes, Father…. No, I don't think we need to worry about him after all."

Intrigued, Pax crept a little closer and peeked around a corner. Zachariah was holding out his wrist and speaking to a hologram of a man, projected just above his wrist tab's screen. Despite his dislike for the bully, Pax couldn't help be drawn towards this new bit of technology. "That is so urbane," he whispered to himself.

"He seems like a total wimp and is way behind in his maths," continued Zachariah, oblivious to Pax's presence. "The entrance exam score must be fake. That, or he cheated."

Hey, that's me he's talking about, thought Pax. *I didn't cheat! There just weren't any questions on stupid trigger-gnomes. Hang on, why are they even discussing me?* He didn't have time to figure that out. He was already late for his lesson. He scurried away and eventually found the second floor of the East Corridor, two minutes late for geography. He received another penalty point and a sharp zap from his torc as he took his seat in room B. The silver device around his neck was beginning to feel very tight and very heavy.

Samuel shot him a look as the screen at the front of the class room briefly flashed up, showing the Judges on minus two points already. Not a great start to the Polls. Pax's cheeks flushed hot. He kept his head down, trying to hide his shame and got through geography without further incident by focusing on his HUD.

In chemistry, he marvelled at the 3D images of atomic structures. He wasn't forced to answer any questions by Sir Kay, much to Pax's relief. When something came up that confused him, he made a note on his screen to act as reminder, so he could look it up later.

After lunch, it was a double lesson with Sir Lancelot and the first-years from Peers. Electronics for the first half of the afternoon. At last, a lesson Pax approached with confidence. When the teacher asked a tricky question that nobody else knew, Pax volunteered the answer, earning a bonus point for the Judges and a nod of approval from his roommate.

The muscles in his shoulders began to relax as Pax started to feel a bit better about his chances of keeping up with the schoolwork. And this time when he asked a question about micro-switches and nano processors, there were no laughs from the other pupils. Sir Lancelot said those topics would be covered much later, maybe not until next term. After, it was computer coding to finish the day. Another subject Pax enjoyed, having learnt how to program Bee-Bop back in the workhouse. He even heard Megan gasp when he nailed a question about sub-routines.

Pax was exhausted at the end of his first day of lessons. It was a strange kind of tiredness – nothing like the muscle aches that accompanied a full day of duties in the workhouse. But he still felt drained, as if his brain had been doing mental press-ups all day. As he and his fellow Judges walked through the canteen, the wall-glass showed the latest headlines.

Piracy in the Thames estuary. The Mayor's approval rating down. Economic troubles.

Pax was too tired to pay much attention. He sat down at the usual table with a thump. The smell of gravy and meat was making his mouth water.

"Enjoying that?" asked Samuel as Pax attacked his pigeon pie with gusto.

"Starving," Pax managed to reply out of the corner of his mouth. "Tastes a bit like Rat-a-tailly, but with fewer hairs. Thank goodness." He scraped at his bowl.

"What are you two doing this evening?" asked Megan.

"I've got so much extra homework to catch up on," Pax replied with a sigh. "Looks like Miss Adams was right."

"You seemed fine in this afternoon's lessons," said Samuel. "Dunno how you know all that stuff."

Pax shrugged and smiled. "Thanks."

"Anyway," said Megan, "you still need to figure out what you're going to do for the talent show."

Pax's smile disappeared and he lost his appetite for bread-and-butter pudding, thanks to Megan's reminder. "Why does it have to be a performance?"

"This is showing your ability to command an audience," Chen said. "Important leadership skill."

Pax didn't want to lead anybody, especially not up on stage. He wanted to make and repair things. Design them, code them, bring them back to life if they were broken. He returned to his room and tried to forget about it, focusing instead on his schoolwork. He looked at all the things he'd been confused about during lessons that morning on his HUD, using his chatbot to understand them. He couldn't afford to be bottom of the class, if he was going to graduate as an Engineer in three years' time.

But the talent show kept nagging away at the back of his mind. The whole process was designed to 'break the ice' with the new senior students. But Pax felt like he was about to plunge into freezing water as he racked his brains for something, anything, he could do to impress an audience.

He was finally able to take off his torc, relieved to be rid of the weight of metal pressing on his neck. His skin felt raw where it had rubbed all day. He couldn't believe it had zapped him. He switched on Bee-Bop.

"Alderman? Are you there?"

"Always."

"I can't believe you zapped me today."

"The teacher fined you. I had to obey."

"Might have mentioned that before!" Pax shook his head. "Now, this talent show, what am I going to do?"

"Whatever you are good at."

Pax heard Samuel coming up the stairs and hurried to end the conversation.

"Well, that certainly narrows it down. Thanks for your help."

"You are welcome."

CHAPTER TEN

The bells of Elizabeth Tower called out across the moonlit rooftops of New London. Pax was getting used to how loud the chimes were up close. But sleep was still difficult tonight. It was the end of the fifth day of term and Pax had been going over his plans time and time again, fighting his heavy eyelids. Now he wasn't sure how late it was. He listened to Big Ben striking the hours: midnight already. Pax sat up and rubbed the metal dots on the back of his head. He swung his legs out of bed, revealing charcoal-coloured trousers instead of pyjamas. As quietly as he could, he slipped a dark hoodie over his white t-shirt.

Opening the drawer in his bedside cabinet, Pax lifted the false bottom to reveal a secret hoard. He reached in and retrieved Charlie's old night-vision goggles, fitting the device over his face. Pressing a button on the side of the goggles, Pax's view of the room glowed red. His roommate, Samuel, was still asleep. Good.

In a tissue-lined matchbox lay the metal body of a headless insect, like an Egyptian scarab broach. The computer lab had just received a delivery of equipment for the new term which meant Pax could, at last, get the final part for his new robot – its brain – and build its missing head. This was Pax's talent, making things.

He'd kept his plans to himself, not telling the others in case they disapproved of his breaking so many rules. He'd had to filch parts from the metalwork lab and sneak into the electronics workshop for two lunchtimes already. It was risky, but in Pax's mind, no worse than coming last in the stupid Talent Show.

Come on, Pax, you can do this.

[-]

Pax crept through the common room, empty and still during curfew. The emblem of a boulder above the fireplace glowed red through his goggles. The door leading to the rest of the school was locked. Pax knew the code wouldn't work at this time of night. Reaching into his trouser pocket, he pulled out a long, thin tool he had fashioned with the help of an old book he'd found in the school library. He slid the device inside the key hole, pressing a button. When it clicked, he twisted the end and the lock surrendered.

Outside, the corridor was cold and unlit. Pax turned towards a buzzing noise that came from his left. He sniffed the air and smiled. That mix of candles and detergent could mean only one thing: polishing wax. Pax had hacked into the school's maintenance system earlier in the day and cleaning droid C-13 was exactly on schedule.

The AI controlling the security cameras knew C-13's timetable, just like Pax did, and had learnt to ignore its movement in the corridor. As long as Pax rode on the back of the machine, he would be safe. But it didn't stop his limbs from shaking.

The wide, squat robot buffed the floor with a circular soft brush on the end of an arm that swept from side to side like an anteater hoovering up its dinner. Pax waited until the machine had pulled level with the doorway and hopped onto its back, crouching down.

For a moment, C-13 wobbled as Pax's weight threatened to topple the machine. A crash was bound to be heard and investigated. With his heart beating in triple time, Pax waved his limbs about, leaning to one side. He leant too far and the robot lurched over to the other side. Another, gentler whirlwind of limbs and tilting. Finally, the robot righted itself and continued on its way. Pax wiped sweat off his brow and tried to control his breathing, slowing it to the hypnotic sweep of the droid's brush.

Once the machine had passed the biology labs and was through the school canteen, Pax jumped off at the bottom of the main staircase. He padded up two floors, his legs already on fire from squatting on C-13 all that time. A shadow flitted across the corridor. Pax froze and then sighed with relief when he saw it was just an owl passing the window. After one final corner, he arrived at the entrance to the computer rooms, wiping sweaty palms down his trouser legs.

Pax pulled from his pocket a coil of wire that had a small magnetic disc at each end. He picked the lock on the door, but when the lock clicked, he left the door closed. He knew that if the metal pads set into the doorframe and the edge of the door became separated while the security system was on, an alarm would be triggered. He slid one of the magnetic discs over the plate in the frame with trembling fingers then prised the door open just enough to squeeze the second disc over the other plate.

"Here goes nothing." He crossed his fingers and let go of the discs, checking they would stay in place by themselves. Pax took a deep breath and opened the door just wide enough to squeeze through. The coil of wire connecting the discs unravelled a little, but everything held in place and as far as Pax could tell, the alarm remained inert. He whispered a thank you to the author of the online article he had found on security systems and stepped over the wire.

Rows and rows of desks, each with a terminal and screen, were laid out before him. But Pax ignored them all. A computer chip taken from one of these would be noticed the next day and investigated. Besides, these terminals had old, over-sized chips that would be too cumbersome for his new robot. Pax went to the far end of the room and entered the teacher's office. There was a cupboard full of brand-new equipment and a box of wrecked screens, tablets and other machines in the corner – no doubt destined for a workhouse recycling centre soon. Perfect.

Pax began to rummage through the box, bringing back fond memories of his time in the recycling labs of Workhouse Five. "This one will do," he whispered to himself. Pax took apart the broken tablet and pulled free its old processor. Then he unscrewed the back of a shiny new wrist tab, one of the best models on the market, and replaced its tiny processor with the old broken one. He carefully wrapped up the new processor and placed it in his pocket before putting everything else back.

When this new wrist tab was handed out later this term and failed to turn on, Pax prayed that the factory would be blamed for providing a dud. And nobody, surely, would check to see if the box of broken equipment was missing a processor. Big Ben chimed out once. 1am, plenty of time for some sleep.

Pax opened the door out onto the corridor and listened. Silence. He glanced in both directions, smiling when he saw no droids around. He stepped out but, in his tiredness, his trailing foot caught on the wire that connected the two security plates. Pax felt something snag and instinctively pulled his foot away.

His stomach lurched as he realised what had happened. As the magnetic disk detached from the sensor in the doorframe, the night split open. Pax covered his ears as a high-pitched siren burst into life above his head. The corridor lights switched on, magnified into unbearable intensity by the night-vision goggles. Pax fumbled to switch off the goggles. Deafened and blinded, he ran for the stairs.

CHAPTER ELEVEN

As Pax reached the top of the stairs, his mind screamed at his own stupidity. Such a silly mistake. He didn't think Bill the security guard could catch a cold, but there might be some security droids zooming his way right now. His heart was beating a rhythm against his ribs in time with the klaxon.

Pax pulled the hoodie tight around his head. His goggles were switched off, but still covered half of his face. He had no intention of getting caught on camera, but if he did, maybe this combination would be enough to stop the security software from recognising him. There was no time for anything better. He leapt down the stairs as sure-footed as a verti-farmer balanced on the edge of a high-rise balcony.

The first camera awaited him, just around the corner, keeping an eye on the school canteen area. Pax couldn't wait for a lift from C-13 again. He delved into one of the deep pockets on the side of his trousers, extracting a catapult and a pellet. It had taken a bit of experimenting over the past couple of nights to get the consistency right, but he had finally managed to mix printer ink, cold porridge and wax paper to form the perfect ink pellet.

Pax crept up to the canteen entrance and, from the doorway, aimed at the camera with shaking fingers. The pellet shot across the room and splatted into the wall, wide of the target.

Rats!

He rushed a second shot, trembling even more by now and landed short. This was taking too long…

He pulled back the catapult once more, squeezed an eye shut and took careful aim before letting fly. The contents of the bullet exploded into a thick, slimy mess all over the plastic casing that housed the observation unit. Some of the black goo dribbled onto the floor below the camera but most of it clung to the unit, completely blocking its view of the room.

Bull's eye, yes!

Pax ran past the biology classrooms and stopped at another corner. With just one shot this time, his catapult blinded a second camera. As he got to the top of the short flight of stairs that led back to the dormitories, Pax heard the sound of rubber wheels squealing over the polished floor up ahead. Not likely to be another cleaning droid. A dreaded security droid.

He dashed back to one of the biology labs and fumbled for his toolset. He fiddled with the lock as the noise got closer, his heart hammering at his ribs. Finally, the door was open and Pax dove inside, pushing it shut behind him as quietly as possible. He sat on the floor, leaning against the door and stretching his legs out as he tried to still his heaving chest.

The rumble of the robot drew closer. Its searchlights shone through the glass window of the door, briefly illuminating the screens at the front of the classroom. Pax held his breath as the droid's movements stopped. And then he realised that the robot was manoeuvring down the stairs. Moments later, the wheels of the droid began to squeak across the floor of the canteen, getting quieter as it moved away.

Pax made a dash for the Judges' common room. He had to splat two more cameras with his pellets on the way but finally he was back. His legs felt heavy as the adrenaline from his raid faded. Breathing hard, he climbed the stairs to his dormitory, before slumping on his bed. Safe at last.

"Where you been?"

Pax's heart started racing again. He sat upright on the bed, quickly removing his mask and pulling back his hood. Samuel was staring at him from across the bedroom. Why wasn't he asleep?

Pax wasn't sure Samuel would approve of his rule-breaking. "Nowhere. Needed a wee, that's all."

"A hoodie and goggles to go pee? I ain't thick, Pax. You're gonna get a load more penalty points for us Judges if you sneak around after curfew."

Pax sighed. He'd never been very good at lying. He needed Samuel to understand. "I've been working on something for the talent show."

Samuel sat up and Pax beckoned him across the room and laid out all the tiny components for his new robot.

"Cor! That is most urbane. How did you learn all this stuff?"

Pax shrugged. "First job I did in the workhouse. Pulling things apart. When nobody was looking, I would put them back together for practice or combine the pieces from two different objects to make something that was more fun. There weren't many stories to read at night so I would borrow books from the recycling lab and hide under the covers, reading up about the wiring, learning the basics of circuitry. As I got older the objects got more complicated. And now I'm here, the machinery in these labs is so much better."

Samuel shook his head, disbelief written all over his face. "Wow. So you plan on what? Doing some sort of display on stage with this little droid?"

Pax nodded.

"Well, I hate to break it to you, but there's been a big clampdown on AI devices these past couple of years after some Peers third-year got caught using one in her final exams. The teachers will confiscate your creation like that." Samuel clicked his fingers.

"Seriously?" Pax thought of all the hard work he'd put in, getting this far. And even worse, the dread of the talent show came back in a flood, twice as bad as before, dousing him in a cold sweat.

"We'll think of summit, Pax. Don't you worry. But no more curfew breaking, OK?"

Pax gave a weak smile and got into bed, exhausted and more anxious than ever.

[-]

Pax wondered why his boat was rocking so much and then he tried to remember when he had joined the Thames Patrol. When he opened his eyes, it was just Samuel jostling his shoulder.

"Oi, sleepyhead. You're gonna miss breakfast."

It would not have been the first time that had happened to Pax. But it was, perhaps, the first time somebody had made the effort to make sure he didn't miss out. He smiled at Samuel. "Thanks."

The canteen seemed noisier than usual as they queued up for food.

"You heard the news?" Megan asked as they sat down opposite her for breakfast.

The boys looked up at the wall screens showing the feed channel. The Thames Barrier was in need of repairs after another storm surge had threated to overwhelm the damn. And in a rare setback, the Council had turned down the mayor's request to double the defence budget.

"Cheery as always. And?" said Samuel.

"Not those. The school news. It's all over Hansard. Apparently, someone was running around in the middle of the night. They broke into the computer labs. Even ruined a few of the security cameras with black glue. Legend!"

Pax tried to keep his voice calm. "Do they know who it was?"

"No," said Megan, her Welsh accent stretching the single word into a tune.

Samuel looked across at Pax and raised his eyebrows as he bit into his jam-covered toast. Pax thought he was going to throw up as his stomach cramped with fear.

The voice of the Headmistress, Miss Adams, blurted out of the speakers in the ceiling, "Attention please!" The food hall quickly hushed. "As you may have heard by now, there was a security breach in the school last night. There does not appear to have been any equipment stolen, so we can only assume it was not a thief but a pupil with mischief on their mind. Let me make this absolutely clear. Such blatant disregard for the curfew rules of this school will not be tolerated."

The screens on the wall of the canteen switched to a grainy picture showing somebody firing a catapult. Pax was relieved to see that his combined hood and goggles had left nothing for the security system to go on. It could be the King himself under that disguise.

"If anyone has information about this wretched person, please come and see me as soon as possible. Until we find the culprit, punishment will be shared amongst each and every pupil. All access to the Gardens will be suspended for the next week. That is all."

A huge groan erupted from the canteen as the mischief maker's status went from hero to zero in the space of a few seconds. Pax wondered if he was safe or whether his time at Scholastic Parliament was about to come to an early conclusion.

CHAPTER TWELVE

Pax spent the day in a daze, shattered from the night before. His neck was taut as a drum, worried he would be called to Miss Adams' office at any minute to be expelled on the spot. And all to build a robot he wouldn't be able to use in the stupid talent show. It took all his willpower to concentrate in class and ignore the fizzing acid that was eating away at his stomach.

He tried to distract himself in the evening by going to the library, but his brain and eyes struggled to focus on any books. Later, as Pax lay in bed, his mind wouldn't rest. Ginger had asked him to show everyone what seedlings can do. But if the whole school saw him fail there would be more penalties for the Judges and more shame for him.

The small window, high up the wall between the two beds, let in a shaft of silvery light. The twins had taught Pax all about astronomy back at the workhouse. He knew that tonight's Moon phase was called *waning gibbous*. It was what happened just after a full moon, but he doubted he could make a talent show routine out of knowing things like that. He heard Samuel start to groan in his sleep.

Oh great, how am I supposed to sleep now?

Samuel's moaning got louder. He started to shout out. Indistinct words at first, but Pax heard his roommate shout 'Dad!' more than once. Pax got up and went over to Samuel's bed. His face was creased in anguish, his skin glistening in the moonlight. Pax shook Samuel's shoulder. The other boy's eyebrows pinched together.

"Look out, Dad, it's an earthquake!" shouted Samuel.

Pax squeezed one of Samuel's fingers until his eyes snapped open. "You were having a bad dream, Samuel."

Samuel blinked and sat up. He avoided looking at Pax. "Was I saying anything in me sleep?"

"A few times you cried out to your dad." Pax sat down on the edge of Samuel's bed. "Is he alright?"

Samuel sat there in silence, not looking at Pax. "It was me sixth birthday," he said eventually. "Dad... He had to work that day. Construction. Works down one of the deep mines, creating new shafts for the kids to use. There was an accident."

"Is he..."

Samuel shook his head. "He was trapped down there for days, along with the rest of his crew. No contact. We all feared the worst, but no one dared say nothing in case it came true. Eventually the rescue team got through the rubble. All of them dead, except me dad. We couldn't believe it when they brought him to the surface. Best birthday present ever. But it was like they'd pulled out a different person."

"What do you mean?"

"Used to be so much fun, always playing games with me and Joshua."

"Joshua?"

"My brother. Dad hardly ever smiles any more. Mum says he feels guilty that he survived. He jumps if Josh or me make a loud noise around the house. How can it be a bad thing he got out alive?"

Pax didn't know anything about parents. But he did know about the dangers of mining. Samuel's story had re-opened the wound from the twins' death. Pax fought back tears. "I... I lost my best friends to a mining accident. If I could become an engineer, maybe I could help make New London a safer place for everyone."

Samuel didn't reply, he just nodded and gave Pax a thin, quick smile.

[-]

The torc rubbed on Pax's neck as he made his way to the canteen the next day, his skin still sensitive against the instrument of torture.

65

"You can get cream from the infirmary. It helps while your skin toughens," said Samuel as he saw Pax fingering the metal necklace.

Pax nodded his gratitude, finally feeling a shared bond with his roommate after their midnight chat. Halfway through breakfast, Pax and Samuel were joined by Megan. She put down her tray and sat opposite them. The boys looked at her meal – dry toast and seaweed juice – and then looked at each other.

"What?" she said. "This is full of vitamins, minerals and protein. Everything you need for a healthy start to the day."

"Everything except taste," whispered Samuel to Pax, who smiled.

"Whatever. How's the practice for talent show going?"

"It's not," said Pax. "I still can't figure out what I can do on stage."

"Ooh, just sing a song or something," replied Megan.

"I can't. I'm tone deaf."

"Not wrong," said Samuel. "I've heard him try in the showers. Very rural."

Pax blushed. *Rural*, the opposite of urbane, was almost a swear word these days.

"Well, that's ten points off the Judges then," said Megan.

"That's not fair," said Pax, as heat flushed across his face in frustration.

Megan sighed. "Anybody who doesn't enter the talent show gets double the penalty for coming last."

Samuel scooped some cereal from his bowl but the spoon stopped halfway to his mouth. "Hang on, brainwave incoming." He looked at the other two with a squint. "What if we form a band? Megan on guitar, me singing and you, Pax, you can play the drums or summit."

"I can't play the drums!"

"They're easy," said Megan. "Nice one, Samuel. A band. I like that. Let's have a practice this evening."

Pax felt the knot in his stomach release. He was pleased Samuel and Megan were willing to help him this way. But he wasn't at all confident about learning a musical instrument so quickly. The show was only two days away now. And he didn't want to let them down. He picked at the rest of his breakfast with shaking hands.

[-]

All through lessons that day Pax struggled to concentrate, too busy thinking about music. They went to the music rooms after tea and sealed themselves inside the padded walls. Samuel switched his torc to broadcast mode and tested out the mic level. Pax hadn't even realised torcs could do that.

Megan picked up a long thin band of metal that glowed with stripes of pink light running the length of the band. She strummed her fingers across the light beams and a harmonic chord filled the room. Pax stared in awe. He would love to have a go at making one of those. He sat down in front of some stout metal cylinders topped with a rubberised skin that hummed with energy.

Megan was great on guitar. She looked funny as she jumped about with her flailing hair, and the music was sometimes a bit too loud for Pax's liking. But it was a proper, thumping tune. And Samuel's voice was as pure as the water from a desalination plant. Pax, however, just could not keep a rhythm going. He always seemed half a beat slow, even when the others stopped and told him just to focus on one of the drums.

At the end of the second song, Pax threw his sticks on the floor. "This is useless!"

Megan combed the hair away from her face and put her hand on Pax's arm. "It's just your first go, don't sweat it. It'll come."

Samuel did not say anything, but Pax could see that he looked worried. They picked another tune, with a simpler part for the drummer but it didn't get any better. Pax knew that he wouldn't be docked points for not participating now, but surely he would cost Samuel and Megan any chance of winning. The guilt sat heavy in his stomach, like an undigested bowl of workhouse gruel.

Finally, Samuel broke the silence. "Mate, think of it like software. I know you're good at that stuff. Each drum has its own

67

stream of binary code. Hit or don't hit. One or zero. You just have to get your hands to learn where the one's are."

Pax looked up and smiled. "That's it!"

"It is?"

"I could programme some electronic drums to play the right notes, and just pretend to play along on stage."

"Not sure you're allowed to do that," said Samuel with a shake of his head.

"Nonsense," said Megan. "Programming is his talent. Pax is just showing that off by pretending to play the drums."

Pax looked at his roommate, hope mixed with fear. "Please, Samuel?"

"I suppose it would be OK," he replied with a sigh.

Pax beamed at them both. "You and Megan wouldn't have to worry about me messing up. You two sound great together. We might even win this thing!"

CHAPTER THIRTEEN

Sir Hector was teaching them history, droning on at the front of class. It wasn't the teacher's fault that its voice was monotonous. But Pax couldn't help wondering if its voice software could be upgraded to something more appealing.

"Well Pax?"

Pax looked up, focusing beyond his HUD. Sir Hector had trundled over and his face-screen was looming over Pax's desk. "Could you repeat the question please, sir."

"Perhaps an hour in detention would help you concentrate in future, boy? I asked you to give me three contributing factors to the Great Divide. Be quick now."

Pax gulped. "Errm, demographics, sir?"

"I'll presume everybody else in class knows what that means. But be more specific. What about demographics?"

Pax rubbed the metal dots on the back of his head, desperately trying to recall the historical novel he had read over the summer. He was sure it had covered this as part of the plot. "Was it too many old people, and not enough workers?"

"Good, now we're getting somewhere. Getting old is very expensive. You need a lot of medical care and nursing, which isn't cheap. At the start of the century, most old people had wholly inadequate savings to fund their retirement. And guess who ended up having to pay for it all?"

"Couldn't the rich people pay, sir?" asked Samuel.

"They could, but they wouldn't. Always found a way out, you see. When there were lots of workers and only a few old people, back in the twentieth century, it was easy to pay for all this. Not now. So, the workers had to pay higher and higher taxes, until they wouldn't take it anymore."

A hand shot up and the teacher turned towards a girl from Chancellors. "Sir, why didn't the government make the old people pay more for their care?"

"Good question. Anybody know the answer?"

It was Zachariah's turn to raise his hand. "The government was always too scared to lose the votes of the old people, sir."

"Correct. Well done, one point for the Loyals." The robot looked around the class. "Well, what are you waiting for? Write that answer down."

Meghan tutted as Zachariah turned to his Loyal party friends with a smile.

Pax remembered something else he had read in the old story, something that had been puzzling him. He raised his hand. "Sir, why are they called *Pinchers*, the old people? Is it true they kidnap children?" He thought of all the rumours that used to frighten Anne, back in Workhouse Five.

"My mum says they eat children," shouted a girl from the back of the class.

Sir Hector wheeled slowly back to the front of the class and then turned to face them all. "Really, there's nothing to worry about. You're perfectly safe here inside London Wall. There hasn't been a kidnapping for years."

The bell rang for the next lesson. Sir Hector shouted out homework instructions as Pax's HUD shut down. He wasn't sure the teacher's answer had been entirely reassuring.

They sneaked in some extra band practice at lunchtime. It went much better this time once Pax had figured out how to code the electronic drums. They only needed to do one song for the show, so it was fairly easy to save onto the machine. Megan taught Pax how to mime beating the drum so it looked as though he really was playing along. He wasn't perfect but his limbs felt energised as concerns over the talent show began to melt. He even started to enjoy the song, admiring his bandmates' skill.

At supper, the three of them were eating together when Zachariah wandered over, along with his usual shadows – two girls and a boy from the Loyal Party.

"Ready to admit defeat at tomorrow's talent show?"

"We're going to wipe that grin off your face when we win, Zach," said Megan.

"Only my friends get to call me Zach, and you're definitely not one of those, Williams."

"Thank the Lord Mayor for that!" she replied.

"You haven't got a chance," he said, staring at Pax, before turning on his heels.

"Why's he picking on us?" asked Megan. "All the first years are doing something!"

"I heard him talking to his dad the other day, in secret," said Pax. "He knew about my entrance exam result somehow. I reckon he's being fed information about his main rivals in the Parliamentary Poll. He probably knows you two are the best musicians in the year. He's worried he might not win."

Samuel shrugged. "The Loyals leave nothing to chance. Win at everything."

"Maybe not this year," said Megan with a twinkle in her eye.

Pax cleared his throat. "I never said thank you."

"For what?" asked the other two in unison.

"For letting me in your band. It… it means a lot."

"That's what friends are for, right?" said Samuel.

Pax froze for a moment. *Friends.* It had sort of crept up on him over the past few days. He had some new friends. He felt happier than a seedling with a slice of cake. And wouldn't it be sweet if the three of them could take Zachariah down a notch or two?

CHAPTER FOURTEEN

T he chatter at breakfast time was full of animated voices. The autumn fog had prevented planes from landing at City Airport for the past few days and, with supplies running low, the kitchens were serving up weak, runny porridge. It should have been dampening spirits but the day of the talent show had finally arrived. Everyone was too excited. Well, the second and third years were excited. Pax played with his porridge, picking up a spoonful and letting it dribble back into the bowl. He noticed some of the other first-year Judges were pretty quiet too.

Megan wolfed down her helping and looked across at Pax. "You not want that?"

Pax shook his head and pushed the bowl across the table.

"Thanks. Cheer up. This afternoon is going to be brilliant. Isn't it, Samuel?"

"Yeah. Reckon we can easily get second place."

"Second?! I wanna win this thing. For the Judges!" She stood up as she shouted this and got a cheer from some older Judges nearby.

Samuel shrugged. "Just being realistic. The Loyals will have bribed the other parties, for sure. They always do."

"What do you mean?" asked Pax.

"Rules say you can't vote for somebody in your own party, otherwise that's all everyone would do," replied Samuel. "But if you bribe enough pupils in the other parties, you're almost guaranteed a win. Look at Hansard."

BeeGirl3>   ZT for the win #Juggling #TalentShow

TheCheftain> Porridge soup, bleugh! #breakfast

Betty363>   Zach odds-on favourite #Loyals #TalentShow

"Oh, forget about that," said Megan. "We'll just have to change their minds with our brilliance. Come on, let's get cracking with our warm-up."

[-]

The three friends waited backstage, glancing around at the other acts. The drama teacher, Mrs Bowie, had pulled names out of a hat to determine the running order. Pax couldn't believe it when *The Robots of Rock* – the name they had chosen for their band –was drawn out last.

"Don't you get it?" said Megan. "It means we're the finale. We'll be the last thing the audience sees before they choose. Bound to get us some extra votes."

Pax just jigged his legs up and down and bit his fingernails. Backstage, it smelt of old, unwashed clothes and he felt a bead of sweat trickle down his temple. The audience in Westminster Hall fell silent as Mrs Bowie went on stage to announce the first act. There was a smattering of polite clapping as Ravi Patel walked up to the microphone. Peering from the wings, Pax could just see the boy from Chancellor's party, pulling out two pieces of paper from his pocket and unfolding them with shaking hands. He cleared his throat.

"The Mine on the Moon by Ravi Patel.
We gaze from London to the Moon
Dreaming of its mining boon
Dug beneath the silver sand
And carved out from a canyon'ed land.
I'm sure you won't dispute this fact
You ne'er did see a finer crack"

As he turned to leave the stage, Pax saw Ravi smirk and accidentally-on-purpose drop his papers. With his trousers low and loose, the whole school got a good look at the top of his bum. And that's when Pax figured out which crack Ravi meant. The poem was about an entirely different sort of moon. He smiled at the other boy's ingenuity.

Mrs Bowie ran on stage half a second later as the audience slowly caught on to the joke and a ripple of laughter turned into a flood. The teacher screamed for silence as she hitched up Ravi's trousers and bundled him away. He protested his innocence to no avail.

"Alderman, one point penalty to Patel for lewdness. Implied or otherwise. I do apologise Miss Adams," she continued as Ravi got zapped by his torc. "Pupils, you will disregard the first act. Really. Our next act is Yolanda, for the Peers, who's going to show us some card tricks."

A pink-cheeked girl came out and showed everyone her pack of cards. She invited somebody from the audience up onto the stage. The boy who came up fumbled his card when she asked him to place it back in the pack. The volunteer had his back to the audience, but from the wings, Pax could see a faint smirk on his face. Maybe he had been planted by the Loyals to deliberately mess things up. Poor Yolanda got flustered when she pulled out the wrong card from the pack. In her hurry to repeat the trick, she dropped the whole pack. She left the stage in tears, with just one person's applause ringing out.

Pax felt sorry for her but also relieved that were now two contenders for the loser's wooden-spoon trophy and that five-point penalty. Maybe the band did stand some chance of winning after all. He clapped as Briony went on stage in a black leotard and cream-coloured tutu. Some light, tinkling music began and all the lights faded except for a spotlight that followed Briony around the stage as she twirled and arched.

Pax couldn't take his eyes off her. He'd never seen such graceful movement. Briony's legs seemed too long and delicate to hold her up but she did not wobble, not once. Her arms swept circles in perfect rhythm to the music as if she were conducting an orchestra. Pax rose to his feet at the end and applauded so hard his hands ached. When he sat down again, he noticed Megan was staring at him.

"What?" he said. "She was really good. And she's in our Party."

"And she's very pretty," said Megan, arching an eyebrow.

Pax felt his cheeks flush and was glad of the darkness backstage. He mumbled a reply but even he wasn't sure what words came out of his mouth.

Next up was Zachariah. There was a huge cheer from the audience as he stepped to the front of the stage and began to juggle with three brightly coloured balls. After a few seconds of normal juggling, Zachariah threw one of them high into the air. He spun on the spot, doing a full 360-degree turn, before catching the ball and carrying on. The crowd, biased or not, were oohing and ahhing, clapping loudly. Zachariah did some more tricks and then replaced the balls with three large knives. The audience gasped as spotlights glinted on the razor-sharp blades.

Mrs Bowie edged onto the stage, her forehead furrowed. Pax could tell she was wondering whether it was safe for Zachariah to continue. Before she could intervene, Zachariah was flinging the knives through the air as if they were soft and blunt, not lethal weapons. He finally took a bow and strutted off stage. He walked straight past *The Robots of Rock* with a wolfish grin as Mrs Bowie tried to calm down the ecstatic audience.

Pax had no idea what the next twenty acts did. All he knew was that they seemed to be taking forever. His hands were shaking and even Samuel had gone quiet and fidgety. Just as Pax was beginning to think this torture would last forever, Mrs Bowie called to the three of them. They were on next. She went out on stage to announce the final act while the three friends got themselves ready.

Behind the curtains, Megan dragged the loudspeaker into position and plugged in her electric guitar. Samuel took his place in the centre and switched his torc to broadcast mode. Pax's heart was beating so hard against his ribs, it could have been an extra drum in his set. He wheeled the electronic instruments into place, opposite Megan and slightly behind Samuel. He flicked the button to turn on the electronic instrument. But as the little screen in the centre of his drums came to life, a message scrolled across.

Factory reset complete. Ready.

Pax stared in horror. No, no, no…

His shaking fingers scrolled through the command screen. Where was his programme? It had been there an hour ago, he had checked it twice. Somebody must have tampered with the drums. If only he'd bothered to finish his mini robot, it could have re-programmed the drums, right here on the spot. Before he could explain to the others what had happened, the curtains were pulled back. He blinked in the bright glare of a dozen spotlights. Behind that wall of light, Pax knew that the whole school was about to see him fail. And he was about to let down his new friends.

CHAPTER FIFTEEN

Megan called out '1, 2, 1, 2, 3' and then strummed her first chord. The notes crashed out of the speaker with a joyous defiance as if celebrating their freedom. Samuel waited for a few more beats as the crowd started cheering. Then he began to sing the lyrics as Megan reined in her riffs. His voice soared above the guitar notes as the audience hushed in appreciation.

The music died down. To his horror, Pax realised that Megan and Samuel had turned to stare at him. This was the part of the song when his drums were supposed to build into a crescendo before the other two burst into the chorus. Somebody in the audience began a slow clap as the silence stretched into a few seconds.

Pax snatched up the drumsticks and tried to beat out a rhythm. He could vaguely remember the tempo. But when his hands tapped the sticks on the drum pads it came out all wrong. Out of the corner of his eye, Pax caught sight of Zachariah hiding in the wings of the stage. The favourite for the talent competition was holding his sides, rocking back and forth. For a moment their eyes met and Pax knew. His drumming got even worse as his hands shook with rage and humiliation.

Megan tried to cover for it, jumping ahead to the end of the drum solo when her guitar kicked in again but that only confused Samuel. He looked at her, puzzled, and then began singing from a completely different part of the verse. All three elements of the music were fighting each other and none of them could figure how to re-synchronise. The audience began to boo. Somebody even shouted 'Get off!'

Megan and Samuel tried to carry on, but Pax virtually stopped. His drum playing became just an occasional tap on the main pad. He worried that his band mates would never speak to him again. He didn't really care about losing the competition, he didn't even care about jeers from the audience. But he had started getting used to having some friends again and he really didn't want to lose them so soon. Were all his friendships doomed to failure?

Finally, the song ended. Pax stood up and ran straight off stage, not bothering to bow to the audience like the other acts had done. The inquest backstage began as soon as the others caught up to Pax.

"What happened?" asked Megan, splaying her arms out wide.

"What you play it live for?" Samuel put his hand on Pax's shoulder. "I thought we'd agreed it was too hard."

Pax just shook his head as he sniffed hard and tried to control his breathing. "It... it wasn't my fault. My programme had been wiped from the drumkit's memory. A factory re-set. I didn't know what to do."

Megan stamped her foot. "What? But that's not fair! You should have told the teacher."

Pax sniffed again and tasted the saltiness of tears. "I knew you'd be better off without me." He hung his head in shame, waiting for them to leave.

"Oh, Pax." Megan put her arm around him.

Pax stood there, stiff as a Westminster statue. He had never been hugged before. The warmth of her arms was soothing all the jagged knots inside his body. He was confused. Did this mean she didn't hate him, even though he had messed up their chances of winning?

"I bet I know who did it," said Samuel not bothering to disguise the contempt in his voice. He pounded a fist into the palm of his other hand with a satisfying slap. "I'm gonna get that idiot."

Pax felt a little less wretched, knowing he hadn't been abandoned by his friends. A dim but vital candlelight in a cavern of gloom. "I saw him laughing his head off from the other wing, watching me mess it all up." He hoped his red eyes and wet cheeks weren't noticeable back-stage.

There was a big cheer from the audience as Mrs Bowie declared that the results had been collected and she was ready to announce the winners.

"Now then school, I will give the top three acts in reverse order. But remember, I said that Ravi Patel was disqualified. It seems that many of you forgot, so Ravi will not be winning a prize. In third place, we have Tristan Beaver with his unique version of the school anthem. I don't think I've ever heard it played on the bagpipes before. Stirring stuff, well done, Tristan! Five points for the Peers."

There was a small ripple of applause.

"In second place is Briony with her wonderful, balletic dance. Lovely to see such grace from one so young. Very good. Ten points for the Judges."

Pax and Samuel clapped and whooped from backstage while Megan danced a jig around them.

"At least our Party got some points," said Samuel as the applause died down.

"And finally," said Mrs Bowie, "this year's winner by a landslide is Zachariah Thomson for his marvellous juggling routine."

The three friends groaned while part of the crowd erupted into a cascade of cheers and clapping. Zachariah came back on stage and bowed.

"The Loyals get to keep the talent plate for the year and, of course, twenty points in the Polls. And Thomson is exempt from the Draft this year."

"No wonder he was so keen to win," whispered Megan.

"As if the Loyals ever finish last in the Polls," snorted Samuel.

Out on stage, Zachariah said something quietly to Mrs Bowie as all the Loyal Party members in the audience clapped and cheered again. The teacher waved her hands up and down for silence.

"I nearly forgot. The award for the act with the fewest votes. I had assumed it would be Patel but in fact he still managed to get more votes than *The Robots of Rock*." She turned to the wings and beckoned them out. "Don't be shy now. Come on out and receive your wooden spoon. And of course, five points will be deducted from the Judges. Remember, New London is no place for losers."

"We will win," chanted the whole school, saluting Mrs Bowie.

The three friends walked slowly out on stage, shoulder to shoulder. Pax looked down at his feet but he heard Samuel whisper something to Zachariah as they passed and saw the sneer he got in reply.

"Now, now, Mr Banton, no sour grapes please," said the teacher as she handed over the large wooden spoon that the three of them would have to take back to their common room in shame. "You really should have practised some more."

"But it wasn't our fault!" said Megan.

"Would you care to explain, young lady?"

"The drum set—" began Megan, but she stopped when Pax grabbed her arm. Admitting to the programmed music might make things worse. "It doesn't matter," she muttered.

"Alderman?" said Mrs Bowie, "minus five points, if you please."

"Acknowledged.

The three friends gasped as electricity coursed through their torcs. Samuel dropped the wooden spoon, Megan yelped as her hair stood on end, while Pax tried to shut out the pain. He'd braced himself for the sting he'd already felt twice before, but this time it was like a giant snake had sunk venomous fangs into the back of his neck. He almost blacked out. The pain ended as suddenly as it had begun. As he hobbled off stage, Pax couldn't feel his toes. The muscles in his jaw ached and his mouth tasted of iron where his chattering teeth had bitten into his cheek.

[-]

The three friends huddled into the corner of the Judges' common room, trying to avoid all the hard stares from other pupils. A few people were gathered around Briony, making sure their congratulations to her for coming second were loud enough to be heard by Pax, Megan and Samuel.

The lights began to flicker as Alderman announced another cyber-hack was affecting London's electricity grid. They were becoming as common as drone raids. Nobody paid it much attention, except for the group whose movie watching was being disturbed.

"Wasn't our fault! Zachariah cheated!" shouted Megan, making Pax jump. Everybody turned to look at them, rolled their eyes, then quickly turned back again.

"It's not worth it," said Pax as he regained his composure. "Just keep your head down, say nothing and people will forget all about you. Worked for me at the workhouse."

"I don't want Judges to finish last, this year," said Megan. "I don't fancy getting expelled."

"Who does?" said Samuel.

Pax rubbed the metal dots on the back of his head. He wasn't sure why, but he felt sure he would get picked in the Draft if the Judges finished last. Fate was rolling a giant boulder right towards him.

CHAPTER SIXTEEN

Pax was just concentrating on a Venn diagram in his HUD when the drone raid alarm attacked his ear drums. Everybody's torcs powered down, and Sir Tristram ordered everybody into the shelters. Pax had to follow Samuel's lead to basement rooms he'd never used before.

The school drone raid shelter was far more luxurious than the one back at the workhouse. There were comfortable chairs, a snack bar and toilets that flushed. But one thing remained the same: a wall glass that winked into life halfway through the raid and the mayor treating his captive audience to a lecture on the dangers lurking outside the city walls.

When they were finally let out of the shelter, Miss Adams' voice blurted out over the PA system. "Would Pax Forby please report to my office."

Pax halted in his tracks as his stomach shrank to the size of a pea. His torc suddenly felt very tight around his neck. This was it. They had finally figured out he was the night-time burglar and now he was going to get expelled. Back to the workhouses and Hairy Hanson. It couldn't have been Samuel who told the teachers, surely? He glanced across at his roommate, who looked surprised but not guilty.

"What's that all about?" asked Megan.

"No idea," Pax lied, hiding his red cheeks by hurrying towards the Head's office.

Best get it over with.

He climbed some steps leading from the lower waiting hall, next to the Eastern Corridor. At the top of the staircase, two medieval armoured guards stood to attention, each holding a sharp-bladed polearm. Pax paused until he realised they were just empty suits of armour, glinting in the sun. He took a deep breath, knocked on the door between the statues and entered.

Pax expected to see a wall glass filled with feeds from security cameras. Or at least a desk glass bursting with whatever digital administrative tasks a headmistress looked after all day. But the dark wooden desk, inlaid with green leather, was quite bare except for a few sheets of paper and the wall opposite was lined with bookshelves. At least a hundred hardback books. Pax almost forgot how much trouble he was in as he imagined browsing through that wonderful collection.

Miss Adams stared at him from behind the desk. "Sit down, Forby."

He did as he was told, feeling sick with nerves.

"I'm sorry that the talent show didn't work out."

The talent show? That was the last thing Pax had expected her to talk about. The lungful of air he'd been holding onto rushed out with a sigh.

Miss Adams smiled. "Everybody has setbacks when they first arrive at Scholastic Parliament. The important thing is to move onwards and upwards."

Pax nodded, not sure where this conversation was going.

"I remember the last time we had a seedling pass the entrance exam," continued Miss Adams with a sad shake of her head. "Poor old Lucia. She made a slow start and as the other pupils began to pick on her, her confidence faded further. It was a blessing, really, when her party finished last and she was expelled. But I'm sure that won't happen to you. There is still plenty of time to turn things around. Plenty of points on offer."

Pax picked at the material in his boiler suit, unsure what point she was making.

"I'm glad we've had this little chat." Miss Adams waved him towards the door.

Pax staggered out, still trying to process the conversation. He shut the door behind him and paused outside, at the top of the stairs. He legs wobbled a bit as relief coursed through him. They still didn't know it was him caught on camera. But there was something about Miss Adams' words that nagged at his happiness, like a stone in a comfortable pair of shoes.

[-]

Over the next couple of weeks, Pax worked even harder than before, determined not to follow Lucia's example. He did extra homework, catching up in the subjects where he struggled.

And when he wasn't doing homework, Pax loitered near the metalwork studios. Any lunchtime they were empty, he worked on his new robot. If Zachariah tried something again – maybe in the next competition – Pax wanted to be sure he'd be ready with a little companion who could do anything.

He had never tried building something so small and complicated before. The workshop had all of the magnifying lenses, tiny wires and fine soldering irons that he needed to construct the metal insect. The textbooks he was able to borrow from the library were far more advanced than anything he'd read back in Workhouse Five.

Just before curfew, when nobody else was around, Pax would show Samuel and Megan his progress and explain which bits he would be doing next.

"You're mad," said Samuel. "It'll get confiscated as soon as somebody spots it."

"Can't believe it's got wings," said Megan, ignoring Samuel's pessimism. "It's going to be great."

"I cheated a bit and included micro rotor blades. So, he doesn't really flap his wings like a proper cockroach would. That would've been too tricky."

Samuel looked at his roommate. "What you choose a cockroach for?"

A shrug of the shoulders. "They have a simple body to copy. They blend in easily. Better for sneaking around the school, spying on the teachers and stuff. There are a few real ones that live around the back of the kitchens. I've seen them. Very hardy creatures."

"Must be if they can live off anything out of our canteen," said Megan

They all laughed. It was the first bit of joy in Pax's life for quite a while.

With the programming finally finished, Samuel watched as Pax turned on the robot in the privacy of their bedroom. Two lights shone from its tiny head. Antennae waggled and then its legs began to move, slowly at first. Before long, it was scuttling around the room. It ran up Pax's pyjamas and rested on his shoulder before spreading its wings and buzzing across the room towards his Samuel.

"Mate, that is wicked wursh," he said as the insect landed on the bed next to him. "What you going to call it?"

"Hmm? Oh, I think he's going to be… Roacher. Yes, that's it." He reached down to pick up the little robot and used a tool to press a recessed button on its belly. "Your name is Roacher," he said. He released the button and the insect beeped. As it crawled inside his breast pocket, Pax felt his heart warm up and it wasn't just the heat from his new metal friend.

85

CHAPTER SEVENTEEN

The three friends were sprawled across some big chairs in the Judges' common room, trying to digest a particularly stodgy steam pudding. Pax was up to date on his homework. Zachariah was so busy basking in the glory of his win in the Talent Show that he hadn't bothered them at all in the past three weeks. If it weren't for the Judges still coming last in the Polls, Pax would be the happiest boy alive.

LOYALS	51
CHANCELLORS	38
PEERS	34
JUDGES	25

A bell rang and Samuel rose out of his seat with a grin. "Well, that's twitching hour. Coming?"

Pax shook his head. Those VR headsets made his head spin, and the alien gore turned his stomach. "Not really my thing."

"Nor me," said Megan. "Fancy a game of Global Chess, Pax?"

Global Chess was played on the strange floating ball Pax had already seen in the common room. It intrigued him, so he agreed. The two friends sat on opposite sides of the sphere as it levitated above a circular stand thanks to a strong set of magnets. Megan let Pax choose which faction. He plumped for Asia, at random, while she was going to be Europe. America and Africa would be neutral in this game. They spun the globe around so the correct part of the world faced them. It was divided into a hexagonal grid, with all the major landmasses in brown and oceans in blue.

Pax had looked up the rules online but couldn't remember them all. "Remind me how the boats move?" he said as they set up the board.

Megan sighed. "Your container ships move two hexagons at a time, in any direction as long as they stick to the blue grid, of course. Your aircraft carriers can move three and carry fighter planes. Your subs move two like the container ships, but you don't have to show them on the map – you just punch in their co-ordinates on the controls so I don't know where they are."

The stand had a control pad built in for each player. Megan pressed some buttons to reset for a new game. After a few more questions, they finally started the game. Megan tried to be kind. When Pax left some of his territories undefended, she pointed it out instead of pouncing. If he forgot to do a trade-run with one of his container ships, she let him re-do the move. But it still wasn't long before she had amassed a fortune and doubled the size of her armed forces. Victory followed shortly afterwards.

Pax rubbed the back of his head, desperate for another go but knowing he didn't have time. "Thanks for the game. I better fetch Samuel before he forgets to do the homework. That maths needs handing in tomorrow lunchtime."

[-]

Pax tried to smile as Samuel told him for the tenth time about his exploits in yesterday's twitching hour, zapping zombies and aliens, and how he'd earned a point for Judges for having the highest score. Their breakfast was interrupted by the appearance of Miss Adams in the canteen. She strode up to the middle of the tables and once the children had all turned to look at her, she clasped her hands together. Her smile, Pax noticed, didn't seem to stretch to her eyes.

"Girls and boys, I have some, err, special news to share with you all. I have just been informed that the Lord Mayor himself will be paying a visit to the school next week. It is a great honour for the school and of course a chance for you all to shine."

Pax sat up straight. Miss Adams didn't seem convinced the visit was great news. Why should that be?

"I want everybody to be on their best behaviour. There will be, I'm afraid, extra duties to help get the school ready, but extra points for the cleanest, politest Party." The head mistress turned and bustled back to her office.

True to her word, the school was a constant flurry of activity over the next few days. The mayor's itinerary was plotted out to the last minute. The classes he would visit were chosen carefully and all the pupils involved had additional homework to cram so they could impress the VIP visitor with their knowledge. Other pupils were required to do extra cleaning duties.

Pax and Samuel had avoided extra homework, but found themselves cleaning some of the storage rooms and tangling with the cobwebs in St Mary's undercroft, just in case the Lord Mayor did a spot check on the basements. The boys had almost finished when the cellar was plunged into darkness.

Pax heard a yelp from the other side of the room, where he'd last seen Samuel. "Samuel? You OK?" He got no reply, but felt his way in the darkness towards the noise of stifled sobbing. "It's OK, Samuel, it's just a power-cut. Probably the Pinchers again."

"Please, Pax. The lights…"

Pax hadn't realised how much Samuel was frightened of the dark. Roacher climbed out of Pax's pocket and illuminated the cellar with his little blue eyes. Samuel was pressed up against a wall, arms wrapped around his drawn-up knees. Pax knelt down next to his friend. "It's OK, Samuel. Look, Roacher's here."

Samuel looked up and gave a faint smile. "Don't tell the others will ya?"

"Course not. Come on, let's go see if you get picked for the drone race."

When Miss Adams had discovered that the Lord Mayor was a keen fan of drone racing, a competition was added to his itinerary. Each Party had to select a drone pilot, and the four teams would have to navigate a course across the rooftop of the Palace of Westminster. Back in the Judges' common room, everybody gathered around, while the third years discussed their choice.

"Why do they get to choose?" grumbled Samuel, recovered now from his ordeal in the cellar. "They're bound to pick one of their mates."

But he couldn't have been more wrong.

"Samuel Banton, your twitching skills are second to none," said a tall third-year girl with a kind smile. "Let's see if that translates into drone piloting. Who do you choose as your second?"

Samuel just stared at her with a stupid grin on his face, until Megan gave him a nudge.

"Oh, err, right, thanks. My second? I choose... I choose Pax Forby."

Everybody turned to stare at Pax. His cheeks flushed red. He stood up shakily, smiling and shaking his head in disbelief. "Thanks, Samuel. Thank you," he whispered to his roommate as people gathered round to pat the two of them on the back.

A chance to impress the mayor and win the Judges some points.

CHAPTER EIGHTEEN

"This course is well 'ard," said Samuel looking at the 3D map that each team had been given for the following day's drone race. The two boys were in the technology lab on Sunday afternoon.

"At least we got out of cleaning the toilets." Pax turned the drone over and used a screwdriver to open a hatch on its underneath. He re-positioned one of the lamps on the workbench to get a better look at the insides of the machine.

"You see who the Loyals chose for their pilot?"

"Don't tell me. Zachariah?" Pax rolled his eyes. He wagged his screwdriver at Samuel. "He's nowhere near as good as you. I saw his score last week on the twitching hour. You thrashed him."

"Yeah well, maybe being picked had summit to do with him owning the best drone in the school. That octacopter is sick. Has to be twice as fast as this thing."

Pax sighed. Every time things started to look up at school Zachariah seemed to be standing in the way. Pax put on some magnifying goggles and reached for a thin tool. "I'll try to even the odds a little. Pass me that coil of wire, will you? Anyway, this is an obstacle course, right? Not just a straight-line race." Pax bent over their drone, breathed deeply and smiled. By the time he was finished, Samuel was getting bored and Sir Brunor was waiting to collect their flying machine. All the drones would be kept under lock and key overnight. At least Zachariah wouldn't be able to sabotage their efforts this time.

But Pax knew that Samuel was right about Zach's drone. It wasn't fair. Another competition that seemed rigged in favour of the Loyals. Before they went to sleep, Pax spoke to Samuel across the darkened bedroom. "I could get Roacher to find where the drones are being kept."

"What for?"

"Well, he could, you know, do something to the other drones. Help even the odds."

"No, Pax. If we start cheating, we're no better than Zach. I wanna win this race fair and square."

Pax felt his cheeks flush red and was glad Samuel couldn't see him.

[-]

Megan wished them luck at breakfast. "Don't let that whelk head beat us again, Samuel. We need the points." She finished her meal and headed off to take part in an athletics' display for the Lord Mayor.

The Judges were still coming last in the Polls. If it stayed that way until Christmas, they would have to do extra cleaning duties next term. And if they were last at the end of the year, well, that didn't bear thinking about. Pax was getting used to school life. He didn't want to end up back with Hairy Hanson.

Samuel looked across at Pax with a roll of his eyes. "No pressure then."

The food hall fell silent as the Lord Mayor entered, en route to an inspection of the biology lab. Pax sat up straight, wondering if the mayor would notice him and say something on the way past. Their eyes met, but there was no acknowledgment or even a flicker on the mayor's face. He strode through the canteen, followed by two armed bodyguards and Miss Adams, who was having to break into a jog every few steps to keep up. Pax swallowed his disappointment. Suddenly his jam and toast didn't taste quite so nice.

[-]

The two friends struggled to concentrate on lessons all morning, grateful the mayor wasn't visiting one of their classes. Pax was wondering if Megan had won the Judges some points in her athletics competition. Samuel looked out of the window, checking the weather and trying to catch a glimpse of the drone course as it was being set up.

Halfway through a double-history lesson, Alderman announced that all drone teams were to report to the start line at once. Pax and Samuel practically ran out of the classroom and made their way to the south-east corner of the school. They began to climb the stone staircase to one of the low towers that overlooked the Thames.

Zachariah came bounding up the stairs and pushed past them. "Out of my way!"

"Oi, the race hasn't started yet," shouted Samuel.

Zachariah turned and grabbed hold of both bannisters, blocking the way up the stairs. He was already taller than Pax and Samuel, and with the advantage of being a step higher, he looked like a giant. "When will you two give up these silly ideas? You and the pinhead are never beating me. At anything." He carried on up the stairs.

"We'll see about that," whispered Pax.

The flat roof of the tower had been decked out with a raised platform covered in carpet and a set of comfortable arm chairs. There were blankets and hot drinks waiting for the mayor and headmistress and a large screen that would relay video footage of the race. Behind the platform the rest of the lead roof had been divided into four sections, one for each of the drone teams. Tall battlements curtailed Pax's view of the city surrounding them.

Samuel and Pax went over to their machine. They saw Zachariah's eight-bladed copter was already hovering, steady as a kestrel, and glinting with menace as the bully went through a check list with his helper. Samuel picked up his control pad while Pax gave the Judges' drone a quick visual check before turning it on. They completed a cross check of all its functions and then waited for the Lord Mayor. It was a cold, breezy autumn day. Swollen clouds hurried across the sky, searching for somewhere to unleash their droplets. Boats bobbed past on the river below.

Pax was shivering a little by the time the mayor arrived. Silas Letherington sat down heavily in a chair and turned to look at the drone pilots. Pax wanted to impress the mayor, explaining how he'd boosted their drone's engines. But as he opened his mouth, a strong gust of wind tugged at the mayor's hair and like the lid of a pedal bin it hinged up and flopped over his right ear, revealing a bald, shiny head. The mayor quickly pushed his wig back into place and tried to smooth it down.

"Well don't just stand there gawping, get your drones to the starting line!"

The four pilots ran fingers over their control pads and their drones rose into the sky. The video screen in front of the Lord Mayor sprang into life and Pax could see that the picture had split into four images – a real-time relay from each drone's camera.

"You concentrate on your control pad screen, Samuel. I'll watch what the others are up to and keep you posted."

Samuel nodded and pressed his lips together.

Miss Adams stood up. "Now then. This is the inaugural Scholastic Parliament drone race. You all know the course. Ten points will be awarded to the Party whose drone passes the finishing post first. And may the best team win." She looked at the mayor for approval, who gave a tiny nod. "On your marks, get set, go!"

The four drones zoomed off towards Victoria Tower. As they climbed in altitude, the wind picked up and Pax could tell that each of the flying robots was being blown off course. Zachariah's heavier, more powerful, drone edged into the lead as they rounded the flag pole on top of the imposing Victoria Tower. The spectators, already struggling to see the drones against the threatening sky, turned to watch on the video screen.

After Victoria Tower, the course dropped down to roof level again, protecting the drones from the strong winds. The pilots had to circle the octagonal central tower. Zachariah was still in the lead, but Samuel was neck and neck with the others.

Pax rubbed the metal dots on the back of his head. Ten points would be enough to overtake the Peers. He wondered about letting Roacher out of his pocket and getting him to distract Zachariah by buzzing past his nose or something. But it was too risky in front of the mayor and Miss Adams. Besides, Samuel didn't approve of such tactics.

Down in one of the courtyards, four landing pads had been laid out. Each one had been marked with a symbol to represent each of the four teams. Zachariah was so confident of the win, he'd started humming a victory tune. He landed first.

"He's not concentrating," whispered Pax with a grin. "He's landed on the wrong pad. Now's your chance!"

Samuel spotted the rock emblem of the Judges and swooped down to execute a perfect landing. Across the roof he heard Zachariah shouting at his companion as if it were their fault he had landed in the wrong place.

At the far end of the course, Elizabeth Tower and the famous clock awaited. The hardest test of all and the only one that favoured the smaller drones. A hoop had been attached to a corner of the roof and each drone had to pass through it before they could begin the dash for the finishing line.

"You're in the lead, Samuel," said Pax. "The Chancellors and Peers are neck and neck, just behind you, and Zachariah is coming last." His voice was rising in volume as he struggled to contain his excitement.

Samuel's tongue stuck out from between tight lips as he manoeuvred the drone through the hoop.

"Well done!" shouted Pax.

"Stop yellin'," said Samuel.

Behind, the Chancellors and the Peers were racing to get through the hoop next. Neither one would cede the advantage but there simply wasn't enough room for both drones at once. They bumped into each other, then skittered sideways and smashed into the hoop, plunging down towards the ground.

"They've crashed, they're out! You're going to do it, Samuel. Come on!"

All that was left was a long, straight dash along the East side of the building, over the Thames. Turning away from the screen, Pax could just about see the approaching dot that was their drone. He was finding it hard not to jump up and down. But then he saw something else. A bigger blob on the horizon. Zachariah's drone had made it through the hoop and was gaining fast.

"Quick, Samuel. Don't let him catch you up."

"I am trying, you know," said Samuel through gritted teeth.

The finishing line was getting closer, but Zachariah's drone was almost level. Despite Pax's efforts in the lab, the other drone was so much faster. There were children leaning out of the Upper East corridor windows, cheering and shouting as the two drones zoomed towards the finishing line. From head on, Pax could no longer tell which one was in the lead.

There was a whoosh, a loud buzzing whine and then it was all over. Samuel brought his drone back to a gentle landing at their feet.

The Lord Mayor stood up and started clapping. "Bravo! A very good race."

After a short delay, Miss Adams was passed a piece of paper with the result. "I declare that the winner is… the Loyal Party!"

Zachariah yelled out and punched the air, as Samuel slumped to his knees.

Pax couldn't feel his toes or fingers, but whether that was from the cold or the disappointment of coming so close to beating that twerp, he wasn't sure. He reached for his friend's shoulder and squeezed. "Bad luck, Samuel. You were definitely the better pilot. He just had a faster drone."

Samuel kicked at a loose stone on the roof and stomped inside. Before Pax could follow him, the Lord Mayor started walking inside with Miss Adams trying to keep up, so Pax had to wait.

"You know," said the mayor, "it would have been much more fun if the drones had had to shoot at some targets or drop some bombs on something."

Miss Adams rubbed her hands and gave a nervous chuckle. "Oh no, your honourable grace. Surely, we don't want to teach the children military matters, not at such an early age. It's bad enough with all their video games."

The Lord Mayor turned to look at the Head Mistress. "We must all be ready to defend our city, Miss Adams. All of us."

CHAPTER NINETEEN

"**C**heer up, Samuel," said Megan as they filed into Westminster Hall with the rest of the senior school. The juniors were already there occupying the first few rows of seats, chatting noisily and squirming around. The Lord Mayor was going to finish his visit by addressing the entire school. The human teachers had all been assigned seats up on a raised platform at the far end of the long, high-ceilinged Hall. The robot teachers were stationed at regular intervals down both sides of the Hall, ready to admonish any mis-behaving children. The banners of the four Parties, with their emblems, hung from wooden poles in between tall, gothic windows.

Pax, Megan and Samuel found their places and sat down together.

"S'alright for you," said Samuel. "Won yer running race. Got the Judges some points. I failed. Again."

Megan shook her head. "You came second. That is not failure."

"And you would have won if Zach didn't have a faster, more expensive drone. You should have let me use Roacher," said Pax.

Samuel's eyes flashed with anger. "Still don't get it, do you? We start cheating and we're as bad as them."

"But the system isn't fair, Samuel. Sometimes you have to break the rules to make things right. Not my fault I never had any parents. Was it fair your dad got stuck down that mine, while Old Leathery gets to strut around London? Eating until his shirt buttons burst? Is it fair—"

Miss Adams stood up and clapped her hands for attention. "All rise please for the Right Honourable, the Lord Mayor of

London." Every pupil at the school fell silent and stood while the mayor walked slowly down the aisle. He showed no self-consciousness in making everybody wait as he progressed slowly towards the lectern, followed by his bodyguards.

Some of the youngest pupils shuffled on the spot and a couple tried to ask a question of their neighbour but were quickly shushed by the nearest teacher. Finally, the mayor took his place and looked up without smiling at the sea of faces. He nodded his head to indicate the school could sit down again.

"Thank you, Miss Adams, for this illuminating visit. It is clear to me that you run this school with a firm, but fair, hand. Your pupils do you credit at athletics, mathematics, chemistry, woodwork and even drone piloting."

Pax noticed Megan was beaming, but Samuel kept his head bowed as the mayor spoke.

"But I wonder if the skills being taught reflect our society? I wonder if the pupils are being shown how to take New London forward, in preparation for the next century and whatever challenges that might bring? New London is no place for losers."

"We will win," intoned the school in unison.

Pax noticed that the smile on Miss Adams' face had turned sour. Her hands balled into fists.

"The single biggest challenge this magnificent city faces, surely, is the threat from our enemy, the Countryside Alliance. I feel that I would be failing in my duty as Lord Mayor if I didn't point out some of the gaps in your pupils' educ—"

The tall lead-glazed window on the left of the speaker's podium burst inwards as a person came swinging on a rope through the opening. Shards of glass flew across the hall, narrowly missing the staff seated near the mayor. Children at the front of the hall screamed and the Lord Mayor ducked to the ground. The Beefeaters sprang across the platform towards the intruder, who had landed awkwardly and was trying to unclip himself from the rope.

The intruder was a skinny young man, apparently unarmed, but with bunches of leaflets in his hands. He vaulted over a diving beefeater and threw the papers across the hall. Most of them fell to the floor in front of the first row of pupils, but a few got caught in the draught that was blowing through the wrecked window.

The man ducked under a lunge from the other bodyguard. He ran up to the mayor's lectern and turned to face the audience. "Make peace, not war," he shouted. Behind him, the mayor pulled out a strange looking gun and with a look of glee, poked it towards the man's back. A blue arc of electricity lit up the hall as the man fell juddering to the floor. The mayor sneered down at the intruder.

A small piece of orange paper fluttered across the hall, like a butterfly on a summer breeze. It landed at Pax's feet, blank-side up. He picked it up, turned it over and read the words.

Talks, not tanks
The pen is mightier than the sword

‡ UKTP ‡

He was about to put it in his pocket when Sir Hector appeared and stretched out a claw. "I'll take that, thank you, Forby."

[-]

"Well, that was kinda odd," said Samuel as the three friends sat in front of a fire in the Judges' common room later that day. There was no underfloor heating in this ancient building but the school was lucky enough to get an allocation of coal from the deep mines and the autumn evenings were beginning to turn chilly.

"You mean the bit when the man came flying through the window, or the bit when Sir Hector told us to forget everything we'd just seen?" said Megan. "Or were you referring to the mayor's speech when he basically told us to get ready for invasion?"

Samuel looked up startled. "What? He never said that."

"Not in so many words."

Pax looked up from tapping away at his wrist tab. "Megan's right. That was a pretty scary speech."

98

"Have you two gone nuts? A man jumps through the window, nearly kills half the teachers with shards of flying glass and tries to hand out some leaflets that instantly get confiscated. I think that's the bit I'm going to remember from this afternoon."

Pax smiled. "Hah, they just told us not to do that, Samuel. I thought you were a stickler for the rules."

"What does it all mean?" asked Megan.

"I've tried looking up UKTP on my wrist tab. The initials at the bottom of that leaflet I saw. But there's nothing on here about it. Not a single entry. I mean you could type gobbledegook into a search engine and it would come back with a partial match or a suggestion for a mis-spelling. But this. Zilch."

Megan looked on her wrist tab. "Huh. Nothing on Hansard either. A boy and a girl get seen snogging and it's trending before their lips are even dry. But this? Nobody is gossiping? I don't believe that for a minute. Something very odd is going on."

"Look," said Samuel. "There's obviously been a clampdown, but why not? Don't want terrorists spreading their message of hate or division, do we?"

Pax sighed and shook his head. "He didn't look like a terrorist. He was shouting about peace, remember? And he wasn't even armed. I'm going to get to the bottom of this."

"You know yer problem, Pax? You're always lookin' for trouble."

Samuel really could be stubborn at times. "Yeah, well, I don't need your help." Pax stomped off to the library.

It was located halfway up the Victoria Tower, directly above the grand entrance used by important visitors to the school. Pax reckoned that even if the authorities had removed any mention of the UKTP from the internet, there would still be references left in books. He leafed through some history and political books and clenched his fist when he found what he was looking for. The United Kingdom Talks Party – a political movement that wanted the Guild of Cities to sue for peace with the Countryside Alliance. They wanted a negotiated end to the civil war. They sounded very sensible to Pax.

As he read, Pax heard snatches of a conversation through an open window. He walked over to try to hear more clearly. It was the mayor and Miss Adams in discussion, down below. Intrigued, he let Roacher climb out of the window and down the side of the building. The little robot relayed the conversation to Pax's wrist tab. He turned the volume down low and pressed it against his ear.

"The Great Divide isn't working," said the mayor.

"I hadn't noticed," replied the Headmistress.

"Sarcasm does not suit you, Cecile. The mines are drying up. The river stocks are dwindling…"

"How long have we got?"

"6 years, tops," said the mayor. "The projections are very clear."

"Then maybe our unexpected visitor has the right idea."

"Don't mention that scum! I will not go begging to his Majesty. No, I have a much better solution in mind."

"But—"

"We must all play our part, Cecile."

Pax heard the door of a hover-car slam and saw the mayor's vehicle glide towards the exit of the school grounds. He rubbed the back of his head. He wasn't sure what all that meant, but it didn't sound good. Maybe the mayor's scientists were working on some inventions to improve the output of the recycling labs, or to increase the yield of the farms. Even find better ways to mine. Pax certainly wanted to play a part in that. If only he could graduate as an Engineer.

CHAPTER TWENTY

The very next day was the first years' field trip to The Wall. Pax dipped his soldiers into a delicious soft-boiled egg and tried to imagine what it would be like, up close.

"So, let me get this straight. You've never visited it before?" asked Samuel.

Pax was relieved to see their brief spat from yesterday had been put aside. "I could see a strip on the horizon, from the top of my verti-farm, but never up close. I've read about it, of course," he said.

"Buckingham Lodge? The Tower?"

Pax just shrugged. "I've told you. I've never been anywhere."

"I first saw the Wall when we moved here from Cardiff." Megan swirled the last of her seaweed juice around in her glass. "It was like a big silver ribbon. Dividing the land from the sky as our train approached the capital, changing colour as we got closer. Pink and orange reflections of the setting Sun. Mum said it looked beautiful but Dad reckoned it was a tragedy we even needed a wall."

"No war, no wall, eh?" said Pax. "That would be nice."

"Come on," said Samuel. "Sir Gawain will be waiting for us."

[-]

The metal geography teacher counted all the first years onto the hover-coach. The streets were busy. Delivery hoverboards bobbed up and down the pavements, dragged along by Lightermen in their orange-and-brown striped uniforms. Pax peered down from his window, trying to see what was being transported. A box of tools heading towards the factory on Albert Embankment. Some bolts of bright cloth, perhaps just coloured by the Worshipful Company of Dyers, and no doubt heading towards the Company of Drapers. Pax even spotted a crate of lemons, with waxy bright skins peeping out from their wrappers, but whether they were destined for the Grocers or the Bakers, he couldn't tell.

There were some points on offer during the trip, so Pax had brought Roacher along just in case Zachariah got up to his usual tricks. But as the little creature tried to crawl out of his pocket, Pax pushed him back down in a panic.

"Stay out of sight," he whispered urgently, starting to regret his decision.

The roofs of buildings on the other side of the Thames shimmered with the autumn sun reflected off solar panels. On the side of a long, low building, a robot was jet-washing some graffiti from the white surface. Pax only got a brief glimpse, but it looked like the same symbol from the protestor's leaflet: ⚡ *UKTP* ⚡ He thought again about the conversation he'd overheard between the mayor and Miss Adams, but still couldn't make sense of it.

When they arrived at The Wall, Pax was shocked to see the scale of the metal structure in front of him. Fifteen metres tall, straight up. A pure slab of vertical, grey steel, stretching off to the left and right as far as the eye could see. Like a giant knife that had sliced across the earth and been left sticking out of the ground. It loomed over him, blotting out the rest of the world.

A smell Pax had never encountered before drifted over on a gentle breeze. There was the odour of hot metal that he was used to from the Houses of Parliament roof. But something else that he could not quite put his finger on was also registering in his nostrils. He breathed in deeply. It was like the slop bins in the canteen, but purer and less sickly, coming from the far side of the Wall.

"Right class," said Sir Gawain, "follow me. Stick close together and don't touch anything." The teacher turned and wheeled off towards a square building that straddled the barrier. "This, of course, is Hounslow Tower. Permanently garrisoned by a platoon from the Defence League. We'll be getting a talk from them shortly. But first, a little race. A taster of their fitness regime. First one up to the top floor wins 5 points for their Party. Go!"

All the students scrambled towards the doors. Tall Zachariah barged his way past smaller pupils, even pushing one of his own Loyal friends to the ground. Pax had been slow to get off the coach so was near the back of the scrum. But Megan had used her speed to go around the outside and was first inside. *Yes, Megan, go!*

When Pax made it to the fourth floor, puffing and panting, he saw Zachariah grinning and Megan sat down, nursing a very sore ankle. He rushed up to her.

"What happened?"

"What do you think? I was winning when that drewgi tripped me on the last flight."

Pax had no idea what a *drewgi* was, but he could tell from the look on Megan's face, it was even worse than *rural*. "Bad luck." He sighed. Another missed opportunity to get the Judges some points, thanks to Zachariah Thomson. He was really beginning to hate that boy.

A captain from the Defence League, wearing a dark green uniform and grey helmet called them all to attention and began a presentation. "London Wall was built in 2040, soon after the Great Divide. The first version was much smaller than this one. And not very effective at stopping the Pinchers from, well, pinching. So, the Lord Mayor commissioned this version. Our patrols go out every hour, armed with the latest weapons ready to defend our city. It's a noble cause, I'm sure you'll agree. Graduates from Scholastic Parliament are automatically enrolled in the accelerated leadership program."

"Where do I sign up?" said Zachariah with a laugh.

"Sign up for death and violence?" whispered Pax to Megan with a shake of his head. "I've seen enough of those in the workhouse."

"Now, we're going out onto the viewing platform," continued the captain, resting a hand on the grip of his holstered pistol. "If the klaxon sounds, it means the enemy is approaching and we'll need to proceed quietly and calmly back inside, OK?"

Thirty-eight voices murmured their agreement.

When Pax stepped outside, his vision distorted and his legs wobbled, as if the ground far below was rushing up to meet him. He was used to heights, of course. But there was just so much space. More than Pax had ever seen before. Up on the verti-farms he could see countless other buildings, but had little sense of distance and no hint of emptiness. Looking west, beyond the Wall, it was as if Pax had spent his whole life stuck behind stage curtains without realising it and somebody had just pulled them open.

Once his breathing had slowed and his vision had steadied itself, Pax started to soak in the details of the land before him. Mostly it was ploughed fields – not everything could be grown in old apartment blocks. There were too many mouths to feed. The crops would have been harvested a few weeks ago. But in the orchards of low trees, Pax could see bright flashes of red apples as the wind rippled across the leaves.

The view would have been quite idyllic if not for the craters. Looking like the pock-marked skin of a teenage suffering from acne, the countryside had been blasted indiscriminately by explosions. The effects of the war. How could anyone prefer that to a negotiated peace? The mayor was mad.

"What's that?" said Pax pointing off to his left at a huge scar on the landscape near the horizon. If the farmland had acne, this was a patch of pestilence. So black, so cratered, it seemed that nature had given up on the area. Pax could see the twisted, crumbling remains of once-huge buildings and towers.

"That is, or was, Heathrow," said the captain. "Used to be one of the busiest airports in the world. One plane every 45 seconds. You could get on an aircraft and travel to anywhere in the world from there. An unfortunate casualty of the early stages of the war. Fought over so many times, until there was nothing left."

Pax tried to imagine all those planes whooshing down the runway, heading off to the furthest corners of the planet. What an adventure that would be! As he tried to picture himself on board a plane headed for Africa or South America, his reverie was interrupted by shouting from the roof above him. All of the class turned and craned their necks to look up.

"Nothing to worry about," said the captain. "Just some of my team going out on patrol."

A walkway had unfolded from the top section of the Wall and four soldiers in helmets and body armour marched forth. Two of them had rifles slung over their shoulders. The first soldier, leading the way, had a pair of binoculars in her hand, while the soldier at the back was carrying a thick pipe that Pax guessed was some sort of rocket launcher. He shivered at the thought of having to use such a weapon.

A bell sounded in the distance and the children looked at each other, wondering if that signified an imminent attack. Again, the captain reassured them.

"That is the sound of the Great Western Gate being opened. Look, if you follow the Wall on your left almost as far as the eye can see, there's a structure a bit like this tower, only bigger. That gate is the only way through the Wall in this section."

Pax looked south, shielding his eyes from the bright autumnal sun, and could just make out the gate. Like two towers stuck together, with a wide road leading up to the space between them. Huge doors were swinging inwards.

"We're in luck," said the captain. "You might want to watch this ceremony."

Pax pulled open the old telescope he used on the verti farms and watched a group of a dozen or so people shuffle through the gate. They all had some sort of bag in their hands or rucksack on their backs. They stopped in the middle of the road and turned to wave at people inside the Wall. Somebody rested their head on the shoulder of their neighbour, wiping at their eyes. The bell sounded and with a great creak the gates started closing. Pax tried to swallow the lump in his throat.

"It's the Long Walk," whispered Megan. "Must have turned sixty today. Banished from the city forever more."

"Will they be looked after by the other side?" asked Pax, his voice croaky with emotion.

Megan shrugged as the band of sixty-year-olds started marching west along the main road. "It's horrible. I remember Nana got chucked out of Cardiff when I was only three. She made the best cakes ever. I miss her rotten, I do."

"Think of it like an afterlife. That's what me mum reckons," said Samuel, putting an arm around Megan's shoulders. "Not a maybe one. An afterlife that definitely exists. One day we'll get to go too. Ain't so bad."

Pax wasn't so sure about that. The people walking away from London didn't seem happy. He looked around at the bombed-out landscape in front of him, the product of all that fighting. It didn't look much like paradise.

CHAPTER TWENTY-ONE

For the next week, every geography lesson with Sir Gawain referred back to their trip to London Wall. Agricultural uses of the doughnut-shaped area just outside the Wall but inside an old motorway called the M25. The transport links that still existed between the walled cities of Britain. But all Pax could think about was that sad-looking group of sixty-year-olds traipsing out of New London forever. It had never occurred to him before how gut-wrenching that switch from insider to outsider must be.

"Why does everybody just accept it's OK?" he asked Megan over eel-pie supper on Sunday evening.

"Don't ask me," said Megan. "I hate it too. Talk to Samuel about it."

So, after he and Megan had played global chess again (Pax won this time), and everyone had returned to their dormitories, Pax did just that. His roommate propped himself up in bed on his elbow.

"That's just the rules, innit? You get to spend sixty years inside a city and the rest of yer life, whatever that might be, in the countryside. Simple as."

"How do those people end up as Pinchers? It doesn't make any sense."

"Maybe they are bitter about being thrown out. Or maybe they get brainwashed by all the rich people living out there."

"They can't all be like that. Why can't people live where they like?" asked Pax, pushing Roacher away as the little robot tried to get his attention.

"Look, it's their fault. They was the ones who built the gated communities. The old people had all the dosh but refused to pay for their healthcare or to have their pensions cut. Me dad said… what was it now? *'The workers wanted their sovereignty back.'* So, they had to split the country."

"I see," said Pax even though it still didn't make sense to him. He lay back in bed and looked up at the ceiling, not really believing Samuel's black-and-white reasoning. Megan's nan, a bloodthirsty pincher? Pfft.

[-]

In the weeks running up to Christmas, things became strained between Pax and Samuel. In a coding lesson, Sir Galahad started making Pax sit apart from the others, giving him more advanced questions and harder practicals to do. When Pax saw that Samuel was paired with Briony, he was convinced Samuel had arranged it on purpose. Pax felt a strange twist in his guts, every time he saw his roommate laughing and having fun with her. He struggled to concentrate as a flush of heat prickled his skin. It felt like he was being punished for being good at this subject.

At night, Pax distracted himself by playing with Roacher and Bee-Bop. He'd built Roacher as a tool to help in the Polls, but thanks to the simple artificial intelligence Pax had coded up, the little robot's personality shone through every day. When they played hide and seek, Roacher started teasing Pax with little sound-effect clues, or sneaking up behind him and tickling his ears. When they read an adventure story together, Roacher used his antennae and beeps to convey the moments of sadness or excitement. Pax thought of him as a little friend more and more each day.

Meanwhile, Pax and Samuel's friendship deteriorated. Pax still thought Samuel was wrong about the man who'd been arrested at the mayor's speech. And wrong to think the rules were always sacred or the Long Walk was OK. A week after the agony of coding lessons had begun, Pax came down for lunch and saw Samuel and Briony together. Pax stared at his roommate, then went to sit on a new Judges' tables with some second years he barely knew. Even though it was his favourite, pigeon pie, the food tasted like ash. Pax's stomach hurt and his shoulders were knotted. He did not want to keep arguing with Samuel. But his roommate was not making it easy.

Megan tried to act as peacemaker. She went along to twitching hour to watch Samuel score more points than anyone had ever managed to do in one term. And she kept playing global chess with Pax, even though he won every time by now.

"Have you tried talking to Samuel?" she asked. "He misses hanging out with you, you know. And I'm getting bored of losing at global chess all the time. It's nearly the end of term. You two should make up before the Christmas holidays."

"You're probably right."

But on his way back to the common room, Pax bumped into somebody he definitely didn't want to talk to. Zachariah was looking up at the Parliamentary scoreboard on display in the canteen. Despite Megan's win at the athletics competition and Samuel's bonus points for being the best twitcher, the Judges were still last.

LOYALS	92
PEERS	71
CHANCELLORS	69
JUDGES	57

"You lot are gonna stay bottom for the rest of the year, I reckon," said Zachariah with a grin. "Can't wait to watch you get expelled in the summer, pinhead."

"We've still got time to catch up in the Polls," Pax replied, jutting out his chin. "And even if we do lose, you don't know the Draft will pick me." He tried to ignore the doubts in his own mind about this. "Could be any of us first years."

"Hah! You honestly think the school's going to expel a pupil from a proper family, when they can choose a pinhead that nobody's going to complain about? Naïve, Forby. Very naïve."

Pax clenched his fists, trying to think of a cutting reply but his brain was too full of fear. What if Zachariah was right? Maybe

Lucia had been expelled at the end of her first year for this very reason? Was that the meaning behind the weird pep talk Miss Adams had given him after the talent show? Had any seedling ever made it to graduation? Zachariah might be making it up to tease Pax, but it could be true. It had a kind of logic to it. He made his way back to the common room as a ball of ice formed in his stomach.

The mood in the Judges' common room was not much better. There should have been smiles on everybody's faces with only one week left until the end of term. But everyone knew the state of the scoreboard. Which meant next term would be full of extra cleaning duties.

And for Pax, there was the added dread of what Zachariah had just told him. "It's my fault for messing up in the Talent Show," he told the other first years as they chatted before curfew, feeling wretched about his performance in the first term.

There was a pause and then the last person he expected came to his defence.

"No, it ain't," said Samuel. "It's Fred's fault for getting caught with a stink bomb on Halloween night. Briony's fault for forgetting her homework last week. It's Zachariah's fault for stopping us from winning. There's lots of reasons we're coming last. We'll just have to try harder next term."

The sense of relief that washed over Pax took away his power of speech for a moment. The ice in his stomach began to melt and the resulting water was threatening to leak out of his eyes. He blinked furiously and tried to smile at his roommate.

"I'm not looking forward to doing the girls toilets." Megan shuddered.

"Should see the mess in the boys' bogs," said Samuel.

"I could try and get one of the maintenance droids to help," said Pax as his voice returned. "I'm sure I could crack the software and re-programme it."

Samuel shook his head. "No, Pax."

Pax wanted to protest. It would be easy to do. Robots were built to make life easier for humans. Surely Samuel could see that? But he didn't want to start arguing again, so he kept his mouth shut.

[-]

After breakfast the next day, they were making their way towards the joy of double maths when Miss Adams walked past them at such speed, the children almost had to dive out of the way. She had her head down, muttering to nobody in particular.

"Oh, this won't do. This will not do at all."

Clutching a piece of paper, she turned the corner towards the Central Hall while the children looked at each other and shrugged. Before they had moved another step, they heard a loud squeak, an enormous crash and screams from around the corner. They ran towards the noise. The scene that greeted them was utter chaos.

Miss Adams was lying flat on her back near the middle of Central Hall. She must have slipped and gone flying because the enormous artificial Christmas Tree that should have dominated the octagonal space had also crashed to the ground. Fortunately, it had missed the Head Mistress but a girl from the second year was lying on the ground with her leg trapped under part of the tree. Her screams were echoing off the high roof. Megan and Samuel ran up to her but they almost lost their balance as they entered the Hall. The floor seemed extra slippery for some reason.

Pax slowed and seeing the other two were looking after the girl, he crouched down next to Miss Adams. Her eyes were closed but she was still breathing, thank goodness. The trapped girl had stopped screaming but gone very pale. When Pax caught sight of the crooked shape of her ankle, he felt a bit funny himself. Samuel was heaving the tree off the girl's leg, while Megan pulled her out from underneath the heavy branch.

Pax turned his attention back to Miss Adams. As he closed his eyes trying to remember the first aid course all pupils had attended at the start of term, he was distracted by the smell of candles and soap. Shaking his head clear, Pax put Miss Adams into the recovery position, trying to ignore the sticky red patch on the back of her head. The paper she'd been holding was on the floor nearby. Pax could see it was a letter from the mayor's office but couldn't read it before Mrs Bowie appeared, scanned the sheet and pocketed it.

"OK, Forby, I'll take it from here." Mrs Bowie knelt down and gave Pax's hand a squeeze. "Well done. Did you see what happened?"

Pax shook his head. "We just heard a loud crash and, when we came around the corner, we saw her lying flat out on the ground. Is she going to be alright?"

Mrs Bowie smiled bravely, but didn't answer.

CHAPTER TWENTY-TWO

After Miss Adams had been carried off by the medical droid, no-one saw her in the last week of term. With three days to go before the holidays, a food fight broke out at lunchtime. Pax couldn't believe the waste of sandwiches and cakes – food any workhouse kid would dream of eating, even after it had been on the floor.

"Did you see what they did to the Christmas tree?" asked Megan, dodging a flying scone.

"I think the toilet roll is actually an improvement," said Samuel. "Looks a bit like snow if you squint at it. Have you seen what's trending on Hansard?"

Pax looked at his wrist tab as a piece of bread flopped onto the table next to him.

> **PunPatel > Miss Adams? Missing Adams more like it LOL**
> **#missinghead**
> **BeeGirl3 > Amnesia Adams can't remember who she is**
> **#missinghead**

"Guys, it's not funny." Pax felt sorry for the headmistress. He had a bad feeling about her absence, but couldn't place his finger on why. Alderman's hologram had taken her place for school assembly and told the school she had taken a nasty blow to the head and simply needed lots of rest.

Sir Galahad spent most of the next day with a piece of paper stuck to his back saying "Virus detected." Despite all the bad behaviour, none of the culprits got caught, no points were deducted for bad behaviour and so on the last day of term, when Alderman announced the scores in the Polls, the Loyals' massive lead was confirmed and the Judges were declared bottom. Megan groaned while Pax bit his nails.

Most pupils would get to spend three weeks at home with their families. Pax had nowhere else to stay, so he was going to remain at Westminster Palace for the school holidays. He wouldn't be the only one. Some parents were needed for important duties in other parts of the Guild of Cities and simply wouldn't have time to take care of their children over the holidays. And some kids who had lost both their parents to the war, such as Chen, would remain at school too. In total, there were at least twenty children who would be staying. They would have the whole school to themselves with no lessons to interfere with their daily routine of fun and games.

Some of the students were envious of those who got to go home, but Pax did not mind in the slightest. The vast building with its library and laboratories, its games room and computers, the long corridors and tall towers to explore was fun when lessons did not get in the way. The human teachers went home, but the robots would be around to look after the pupils. And best of all, Pax wouldn't have to wear his torc for three weeks. A chance for the calloused skin around his neck to recover.

Samuel was packing his things in the dormitory, getting ready to leave.

"I hope you have a nice break," said Pax.

"Cheers. You too."

Pax opened the drawer next to his bed and handed Samuel a small box.

"What's this?"

Pax shrugged. "A little present. To say sorry for arguing." He crossed his fingers behind his back, hoping Samuel would like it.

Samuel shook it and heard a solid object rattling inside. "What is it?"

"Something I made. Open it and see."

"Didn't get you anything," said Samuel as he pulled the lid off and peered inside. As the lid came away a glow of blue light emerged. Samuel picked up something the shape and size of a smooth, large pebble. He turned it over and over in his hands.

There was a metal band running around the middle while the top and bottom were made of curved plexi-glass.

Samuel cupped his hands around it. "Here, it's warm." He could not take his eyes off the neon blue that radiated from his present. It started to fade.

"Give it another shake. The light and warmth will come back," said Pax. "It should fit in your pocket easily enough. If you're ever somewhere dark, just take it out and shake it."

"Thanks, mate, that is urbane!"

"Glad you like it." The two boys stepped closer together and reached out their hands to shake before stuffing them back into their trouser pockets. Pax breathed a sigh of relief. Hopefully they could go back to being best friends in the new term.

[-]

Pax spent the first few days of the holidays worrying about the Polls. How could he find out if Zachariah's claim was true? There must be school records he could check somewhere. There was still no sign of the Head, so Pax risked sneaking along to her office on the third morning of the holidays.

He couldn't unpick the lock to her office for some reason, so Roacher scuttled under the door with instructions to look for a computer he could dock into and search. But when Roacher came back out a few minutes later, he flew onto Pax's arm and slowly shook his antennae.

Pax tried the library. He found a record of all the pupils who had passed the entrance exam and all those who had graduated from school. It was painstaking work, but by comparing the lists Pax could figure out which pupils had not lasted the three years. He checked the families of those expelled and breathed a sigh of relief when he saw the results. Out of the twenty pupils expelled in the past ten years, three had been seedlings, ten orphans and seven from ordinary families. Seedlings were the least likely to be picked. Zachariah had been lying, making him worry over nothing.

He wandered back to the Loyals' common room, happy with his findings. But something was playing at the back of his mind. Had he missed something? He was so pre-occupied he lost at global chess to Sukhwinder, whose parents were away, working in Glasgow.

"Sukhwinder, you've covered probability in maths lesson, right? As a second year?"

The other boy nodded.

"I've been trying to work out who's mostly likely to get expelled, if Judges finish last at the end of the year. I have a list of all the pupils expelled over the past ten years. You want to see?"

"Sure." Sukhwinder looked at Pax's sheet of paper with the numbers written down. "So, you think the Draft might not be random? Very interesting, actually."

"I just wanted to check. As a seedling, I'm the least likely to get picked, right?"

Sukhwinder looked at the paper again and shook his head. "Actually, you need to know how many seedlings attended school during those ten years."

Pax gulped as he called up the list of pupils who'd passed the exam on his wrist tab. "There've been only three."

Sukhwinder pulled a face. "Then I'm sorry to say I don't fancy your chances. If we remain last in the Polls, there looks to be a 100 percent chance of you being picked."

Zachariah had been right. Pax was going to get expelled in the summer unless there was a big turnaround in the Judges' fortunes. He stared at the chess globe in front of him. His hopes of becoming an engineer seemed to be drifting out of reach.

116

CHAPTER TWENTY-THREE

Although there was little tolerance for any of the major religions in New London after the Great Divide, the tradition of swapping presents near winter solstice had been maintained to promote the ethos of sharing. That special morning was still known as Christmas by most people. It was marked in the school with a lovely bread and butter pudding for breakfast. It did little to cheer up Pax. He could see his breath in front of him. The Palace of Westminster was a fine building but it was old and too big to heat properly during the holidays. Precious coal was not to be wasted. One of the girls had come down to breakfast in her coat and most of the others had on a hat or gloves.

They gathered in the central hall around the Sharing tree where Miss Adams had fallen so spectacularly a couple of weeks ago. Underneath the tree this time was a pile of presents provided by absent parents or other relatives. As a seedling, Pax had occasionally swapped little nick-nacks with his friends but had never before had to witness the good fortune of others. It didn't improve his mood.

Bradley, a third year from Chancellors, started going through the parcels, calling out the name on each label and passing it around. The pile had almost disappeared when Pax heard his name called out. At first, he assumed he had mis-heard, but when Bradley repeated his name again, Pax moved forward and took a small, bright green box. It was so light, Pax wondered if it was empty.

Who was it from? There was no label. He tried to savour the moment, but his fingers trembled with excitement and his chest fizzed with joy. He couldn't resist tearing open the parcel. At first, he thought the box really was empty but when he tipped it upside down a tiny grey cube fell out. He picked it up. It was surprisingly heavy. He found a raised disc on one of its faces and pressed. The opposite face of the cube opened up and beams of light shone out, dazzling Pax's eyes. He blinked and held the cube on his outstretched palm.

The light was forming a hologram of him, Samuel and Megan. He smiled as he remembered Megan taking the picture just before the end of term. He pressed the button again and a different holographic picture appeared – the three friends practising for the talent show. Those smiling faces seemed so innocent, not aware of the disaster about to befall them. If only he could go back in time and warn them all.

Another press of the button and a final image materialised. The three of them grinning on the viewing platform at the Wall. He remembered Megan taking that one too. The present must be from her. His happiness was tarred by a feeling of guilt – he hadn't got her anything. He suddenly wished he could see his friends again, right now.

"Ahh, a holoframe," said Bradley looking over at Pax's present, "nice."

Pax wiped a tear from the corner of his eye and just nodded.

[-]

In the days between Christmas and New Year, Pax played global chess with Sukhwinder almost constantly. The older boy had explained there was a big tournament on next term with the winner gaining lots of points. It would be a good chance for the Judges to catch up in the Polls, an opportunity Pax couldn't afford to miss now he knew for sure what would happen if they remained in last place. With a decent opponent to practice against, he improved quickly. After a few games with Sukhwinder, he won every time, as long as he concentrated.

It was one morning on a particularly cold and smoggy Wednesday, while Pax was walking the corridors trying to keep warm, that he caught a whiff of floor polish and for some reason thought of Miss Adams. He realised he still had not seen her since the accident. Unlike the other human teachers, the Head lived at school. She was taking a long time to recover. Pax went to the infirmary. The medical droid on the reception desk swivelled its head to look at Pax. "May I help you?"

"Errm, yes. I was wondering if Miss Adams was still in the infirmary?"

"I am not at liberty to say."

"But is she OK? She's not lost her memory, has she?" Pax was beginning to worry that the sick joke about the Head was true. She was scary and strict, but she had shown kindness to him. To lose your memory, your identity, just because of a slippery floor. That wasn't right.

"I am not at liberty to say."

Pax tutted. "Well thanks for your help." He turned and walked away.

As he reached the end of the corridor, he noticed one of the security cameras with its little red light beneath. Nobody else was around. "Alderman?"

"Yes, Pax?"

"Do you know what's going on with Miss Adams?"

"I am not at liberty to say."

"Oh, don't you start!"

[-]

On New Year's Eve, Pax had beaten Sukhwinder at global chess for the third time that day, when the older boy looked at his wrist tab.

"You coming to watch the fireworks? They're starting in five minutes."

"Sure." Pax breathed out and smiled. "That sounds like fun." He'd watched the city's fireworks before, at the workhouse – the one night of the year seedlings were allowed to stay up late – sharing in the celebration with all the workers.

They made their way to the rooftop along with a dozen other pupils. Pax's coat was a thin school-uniform jacket. He was the only one there not wrapped up warm. But somebody handed him a mug of hot chocolate and he gratefully wrapped his hands around it. He looked up to see who had been kind and looked straight into the eyes of Briony. Pax nearly dropped the mug.

"Hi," she said.

"Oh, hello. I didn't know... I didn't realise you'd stayed up over the holidays."

She shook her head. "I went home for a bit, but Mum had to go off on some project and Dad's always too busy."

"Right," said Pax. "You're lovely here. Err, I mean it's lovely that you're here. To watch the fireworks. Umm, thanks for the drink."

Briony giggled. "Look. They're starting."

Pax spent fifteen wonderful minutes standing next to her. The drink had quickly lost its warmth and he was freezing cold but he wasn't going to budge until the firework display was over. As the pupils on the roof gazed up at the explosions of light, Pax could feel the thud of the rockets through his chest. Even when the fireworks weren't going off, his heartbeat raced and fluttered. He kept trying to steal glances at Briony's face when everyone else's attention was fixed firmly on the cascade of coloured stars across the water.

Afterwards, he followed Briony and Sukhwinder back to the Judges' common room. Pax wanted to talk to Briony all night long, but his tongue felt awkward and he couldn't think of much to say. Sukhwinder was much better at talking to her. Pax barely said a word. His cheeks grew tired from grinning so much. After Sukhwinder shared out some sweets he'd received for Christmas, Pax went to bed still smiling. It had been the best New Year's Eve ever.

[-]

In the last few days of the holiday, Pax revised harder than ever, determined to score extra points in next term's lessons and help the Judges catch up in the Polls. He found a book in the library called *Play Better Global Chess* and memorised all the strategy tips. He tried to get to know Briony a bit better too over meal times, but his brain kept fogging over and his tongue always felt too big.

Finally, the other pupils arrived with their luggage for the start of term. The wonderfully wide school corridors were once again noisy, crowded spaces where Pax had to stick to the proper side of the dividing line. Friends were excitedly telling each other about their holidays, the presents they had received or the parties they had enjoyed.

Pax was playing with Roacher on his bed when Samuel returned.

"Hiya Pax. How was yer Christmas?"

There was so much to tell his roommate, but Pax didn't know where to begin "Alright thanks. Yours?"

"Mate, I'm sorry about not messaging you more. Me holiday got… complicated."

Pax had been so wrapped up in finding out about the Draft, revision, chess practice and Briony, he'd barely noticed the lack of messages. "That's OK."

"Brought you a present."

Pax looked up. "Really?"

"I'm pretty rubbish in the kitchen, so Mum baked them." Samuel handed Pax a box tied with a ribbon.

Pax undid the bow and lifted the lid. A row of biscuits, all shaped like cockroaches, were lined up in the box. They each had chocolate chips for eyes and fine lines of icing for wings. "Wow, they look delicious. Want one?"

Samuel shook his head as Pax took a biscuit and bit into it. It was soft and buttery with just enough sweetness from the decoration. Pax used to think the school canteen food was pretty amazing, but he had never tasted a snack as nice as this. It was like one of those lovely warm dreams you never want to wake up from.

If those biscuits were dreamy, the start-of-term assembly was a cold, hard wake-up call. The normally radiant stained-glass windows and gold-leaf detail on the furnishings of the grand debating chamber were dull and flat. The early January daylight leaked into the great room as if it were embarrassed to be there.

The once-Royal Throne at the head of the chamber was a magnificent chair surmounted with a crown, little statues of angels on either side and, behind, a wall of gold and heraldic symbols shaped like a miniature version of the whole palace. But it was empty. There was still no sign of Miss Adams.

Alderman's voice boomed out of the speakers. "Quiet please. Thank you. As you will have noticed, Miss Adams is still unable to resume her duties. While she continues to recuperate, I will be in charge of running the school."

Pax began to smile – maybe this term would be easier for him after all.

"Do not," continued Alderman, "for one minute, think this gives you an excuse to start messing around and talking to your neighbour, LIGHTWOOD! Yes, you boy. I can see everything that goes on and bad behaviour will not be tolerated."

Pax's smile disappeared. All of the pupils sat upright and stopped fidgeting while Lightwood, a second-year Chancellor, looked like his ears might pop, they had gone such a violent shade of red.

"The Lord Mayor thinks your standard of education has been slipping. So, there will be extra homework and more *discipline*."

Pax gulped, feeling the weight of his torc pressing heavy on his neck once more.

CHAPTER TWENTY-FOUR

"**T**his is not good," said Pax as the three friends made their way to their first lesson of the term – physics with Sir Percival.

"Yeah, Alderman sounds like he's going to be even stricter than Miss Adams," replied Megan.

Before the physics class had even sat down, one of Zachariah's groupies had been deducted a point for talking too loudly on the way into class. He soon shut up as his torc administered a punishment. This never happened to a Loyal. A few minutes later, Sir Percival asked Megan a question on electromagnets, which they hadn't even been taught yet.

Her forehead creased in confusion. "I'm sorry, sir, I don't know."

"One point penalty for the Judges. Alderman?"

"Acknowledged."

Megan gasped in pain as she was zapped by her torc. Pax put his hand up to supply the correct answer, having read ahead on this topic during the holidays but Sir Percival was not interested in giving out bonus points.

In their history lesson, Sir Hector taught the pupils about the great battles of the Napoleonic Wars – Waterloo and Austerlitz – even though they weren't on the curriculum for that term. But it was obviously a favourite subject for Zachariah who sat up smiling throughout the lesson, answering lots of questions on the tactics Napoleon had used and what he had done wrong in attacking Russia.

By lunchtime, it seemed clear the Knights of the Round Table had changed personality. Opinion was divided on this new style of teaching. The first-year Loyals took their cue from Zachariah who declared that Alderman obviously had the right idea about how to run a school. Even though the Loyals had lost some points that morning, the other Parties had also been caught out by the stricter regime.

"At least everyone is losing points, now," joked Samuel.

Pax didn't laugh. He needed the Judges to gain points so they could catch up in the Polls or he was out of here. Over the next few days, the running totals in the Polls started going down as more and more pupils lost points for very minor misdemeanours and few bonus points were awarded.

Even worse, all that extra revision Pax had done over the holidays turned out to be a waste of time. He never got to demonstrate his new knowledge as the lessons continued to veer off the list of topics they were supposed to cover and started to include far more military references.

Chemistry lessons talked about the formula for dynamite and other explosive materials. Biology gave gruesome details of what happened when a human breathed in a nerve agent. One of the girls fainted when the class was shown a video of a goat being exposed to something called Anthrax.

The three friends were clearing up in the kitchens at the end of the first week – part of the Judges' punishment for being last in the Polls before Christmas – when Pax finally told the others what he'd found out during the holidays. He hadn't wanted them to feel sorry for him, but he couldn't hold it in any longer. At least they wouldn't have to worry about the Draft if the Judges remained last for the rest of the year.

"But that's not fair," said Megan. "They can't pick you for expulsion just because you're a seedling."

"We'll just have to make sure the Judges don't finish last," replied Samuel.

"That won't be easy with this new style of teaching," said Pax.

"All Alderman's fault, I reckon," said Samuel.

Pax shook his head. "He's probably just following orders from the mayor. He's the one obsessed with war. Making these changes to the curriculum while Miss Adams isn't around to stop him."

"Hey, you don't suppose Old Leathery *caused* her accident," said Megan. "Do you remember how slippery it was when she fell?"

Pax thought back and suddenly could smell candle wax and soap again. "There was too much floor polish. Of course!"

"So?" said Samuel. "Probably just a glitch with a cleaning droid."

"Or somebody had re-programmed it," replied Pax.

"Can't you two hear yourselves?" said Samuel. "The mayor planned this all out? Really? First of all, he is our elected leader, so why shouldn't he change school lessons if he wants? Second, how could he have known she'd be out of action for this long, just because of a fall. It's just bad luck she hasn't recovered yet."

Pax wasn't convinced. So later that night, as the cleaning droid C13 was passing the Judges' common room around midnight, Pax encouraged Roacher under the locked door. The little robot came back a few minutes later, having downloaded a log of the cleaning droid's activity. Unfortunately, it only went back to the start of the month. Any possible evidence of tampering from last term had been wiped clean. So, the mayor's possible involvement remained nothing more than an uncomfortable nag at the back of Pax's mind.

In the meantime, there were toilets to clean, bins to be emptied and lessons in warfare. To cap it all off, the weather was appalling. There were none of those clear, bright skies that brought hard frosts and a welcome hug of sunshine. There wasn't even snow or ice to enjoy in the Victoria Tower Gardens. The grey clouds never seemed to leave them alone. The sky was always dreary and slightly damp, like a soggy dishcloth after washing up too many pots and pans.

The final shock of the month came when the geography teacher told the first years they were returning to London Wall. And this time they would be venturing outside to help harvest the winter vegetables.

"But, sir," said Samuel. "We ain't supposed to go beyond the Wall until we're in the third year."

"Well rules change, Mr Banton. The third years are too busy shadowing the Defence League. And we can't let those crops go to waste."

Pax looked around the room, wondering if he was the only one thinking the obvious. "Won't it be dangerous, sir? You know, outside the Wall?"

"Relax, Forby. The farm at Osterley Park hasn't been attacked for years. Besides, you'll have drone cover to keep an eye on things. Really, I thought you were braver than that, young man."

Zachariah made a noise like a chicken clucking and his friends joined in the mockery.

CHAPTER TWENTY-FIVE

After two more days of chicken impressions followed him around the school, Pax was getting ready for the trip to Osterley Farm. He looked out of the window to check on the weather. No sun, no snow, in fact almost nothing. Pax could barely see the far side of the Thames. Thick fog wrapped itself around the school like the hug of a dead polar bear.

He went up to his dormitory to put on a thick pair of socks and an extra t-shirt underneath his school boiler suit. The extra clothes didn't stop him from shivering. Samuel was already there, also getting wrapped up for their trip.

"Hey, do you think I should bring Roacher with me?" asked Pax.

"What for?"

Pax shrugged. "Zachariah's been very quiet recently. If I know him, he's bound to try some new trick on us soon. We might need a little help, watching our backs."

"OK. But don't let the teacher catch you with that thing. The way they've been this term, you'll lose about a hundred points for the Judges!"

On the journey towards the West Gate, Pax paid less attention than last time to the sights of New London that were flashing past the hover-bus windows. He picked at a loose thread on his coach seat as he thought about going into the Neutral Zone. He felt sure Miss Adams would not approve if she were around to witness this.

Samuel was not being much help in calming his friend's nerves. He had been selected to pilot one of the drones that would keep the class safe while they collected the vegetables. He sat at the front of the bus, with a big grin on his face, receiving instruction on the surveillance work.

Megan talked to Briony and every time Pax turned around to say something, he lost his nerve and turned back again. Why was it so difficult? He didn't have a problem chatting with Megan. But whenever Briony was nearby, his tongue felt numb and the inside of his head went fuzzy.

The sooner we get on with collecting this harvest, the better, thought Pax. At least there were points on offer to the team who collected the most. And maybe Pax's experience on the verti-farms would help the Judges begin to catch up in the Polls.

[-]

The Western Gate, up close, was even more impressive than Hounslow Tower. A huge steel archway curved between two strongholds. At first, Pax had thought the chief guard and all his team were small and insignificant, like ants crawling around next to a normal-sized door. But as the hover bus approached the archway and stopped, he could see that the sentries were tall and broad, clad in body armour and visored helmets. They only looked small in comparison with the enormity of the gate.

As Pax tried to swallow down his nerves, the bus driver spoke with a guard who turned and gave a signal to an unseen colleague. Somewhere within the gateway giant cogs began to turn. The children jumped when the mechanism started to prise apart the huge doors with the noise of a giant boulder being dragged across a floor.

Slowly, the crack in the doors expanded. Everyone in the bus craned their necks to look at the broadening view of the countryside but the morning's fog seemed worse beyond The Wall. The road quickly disappeared into banks of wispy cotton wool. The bus driver said one final thing to the chief guard and then they were off, passing under the archway and out into the great unknown. Pax's legs jigged up and down and everyone around him fell into a nervous silence.

The vehicle followed the road for ten or fifteen minutes. It snaked through derelict buildings, past ancient trees that looked like huge skeletons. Pax caught glimpses of man-made reservoirs, where the fog seemed thickest of all. After several twists in the road, Pax lost all sense of direction. The bus driver stopped.

"Everybody out," said the teacher.

As they disembarked each pupil was given a backpack with an open top to act as a basket and a digging tool to help them collect the vegetables. The drone pilots were handed their control pads and assigned to a group of children. Pax was pleased to see that he was in the same team as Megan, Briony and Chen with Samuel as their drone pilot. The flying machines began to buzz like angry wasps as the pilots checked their controls.

The teacher addressed Pax and the other Judges. "Right, team A. You've got 90 minutes to harvest all the carrots in the second field." Sir Gawain's chest lit up with a map of Osterley Farm and he indicated which field this was and where the bus would be waiting for them.

The students studied the map and turned to look for their field, but it was impossible to see because of the fog. Once Samuel had got his drone hovering about twenty metres above their heads, he programmed their destination into its flight path and the pupils trudged off, following the drone.

"What's the view like, up there, Samuel?" asked Megan.

"Just as bad as down here. Fog bank extends up at least as far as the drone."

"I guess the Pinchers won't be able to spot us at least," said Pax looking around at the frosted fences and dew-covered spider webs. He was trying to cling onto some optimism about this task. Winning a few points for the Judges would be very welcome about now.

[-]

The second field seemed rather big for just four of them. Rows upon rows of green tufts sticking up in raised lines. And between the rows, thick, damp soil that stuck to the children's boots like chocolate glue. Pax showed the others the quickest way to loosen the soil with a fork and ease the carrots out, keeping the root and top intact. They took a line each and started the back-breaking work. Pax went too fast to begin with, desperate to collect the most, but he soon began to puff and had to slow down.

After twenty minutes, Samuel shouted across the field. "Err, I think there's a problem with the drone. The picture's just cut out." He looked at the control pad. "What the heck?" Samuel jumped out of the way as the flying machine descended from the fog and crashed into the soil. Two of the rotor blades pinged off and zinged past Megan's head. The body of the drone sank into the crater of mud it had created and began to smoke.

"Nearly gave me a haircut!" shouted Megan. "What did you do?"

"Nuthin! I sent it up above the fog bank. There was a bit of movement on the horizon before the picture went bright red. Then it cut out and the drone just fell."

"A drone malfunction, that's just great," muttered Pax.

Everyone else stopped collecting carrots and ran over to see what was left of the machine. They called him over. Cursing the delay, Pax came to peer at the wreckage. A hole in the middle of the drone's body had crinkled, black edges as if somebody had sliced through the metal casing with a diamond drill. His breathing quickened and his throat constricted as Pax realised what he was seeing. "Umm, this wasn't a mechanical failure." He looked at the other four. "This drone has been shot down."

Megan and Chen gasped. Briony started to ask "Who would do…"

The girls looked at each other and replied in unison. "Pinchers!"

Pax staggered back. He hadn't wanted to believe the Pinchers could be as bad as the rumours suggested, but maybe he had been wrong all along. Freezing fog crept into his mind as doubts sent shivers down his back.

Samuel breathed in a big lungful of air and shouted "Help!" at the top of his voice.

"Don't do that," said Pax. "They'll hear us."

"But how are the others going to know we're in trouble? They won't come to rescue us if they don't know we're being attacked," said Chen.

Pax shook his head. "They might be under attack too. We have to get back to the bus as fast as possible."

"We haven't got the drone to follow no more," said Samuel, his voice all tight.

Chen looked at her wrist tab and tapped the screen. "No signal."

They looked around the field. The fences all looked the same, especially with the backdrop of fog obscuring their view towards the horizon.

Briony clung onto Megan. "I'm scared." Tears began to roll down her cheeks and Megan tried to smile while squeezing her shoulder.

Pax felt something crawling over his trouser leg.

Briony screamed and pointed. "Urghhh!"

Pax was about to really freak out when he realised it was only Roacher. The little robot must have woken itself. "It's OK, Briony, it's my pet. Long story, but don't worry. It's on our side." Pax scooped up Roacher in his hands and brought the robot up to his face. "We need your help, little buggy. Can you show us the way back to the bus?"

Roacher flicked his antennae up and down. He unfolded his small wings and with two thin beams of blue light shining from his head, Roacher took off, flying along one of the paths that led from the field. Everybody turned to follow. Pax still didn't want to believe Pinchers were behind the attack, but the evidence seemed pretty clear. And he really didn't want to risk finding out for sure right now. He just hoped they could get back to the bus as quickly as possible.

Assuming the bus was still there…

CHAPTER TWENTY-SIX

The five children scurried through the mist, following Roacher's light as if they were moths drawn to a blue candle. When Samuel scuffed his boot on the ground the sound seemed to multiply, echoing off the fog. They all stopped and listened for a reaction. Who knew how close the Pinchers were? Lurking just out of sight or maybe miles away by now, having already achieved whatever they had set out to do? Not knowing seemed even worse than seeing a Pincher, evil or otherwise.

The route back to the bus seemed to last hours. Pax could hear Briony's teeth chattering and she kept rubbing her gloveless hands together. "Hey, Samuel. Lend Briony your glow stone, will you? It will help keep her hands warm."

"I can't."

Pax rolled his eyes. "Did you leave it back at school? You're supposed to keep it with you. Pocket-sized for a reason."

"Keep your voice down," said Megan.

"I don't have it no more," whispered Samuel.

"BUT—" Pax clamped his hand over his mouth to stop himself from shouting. The present he had made especially for Samuel. *There's gratitude for you.* Pax tutted and took off his gloves to give to Briony. She smiled.

Creeping along and stopping to listen for noises, the group made slow progress. Pax's legs ached with all the tension and his head ached as his ears strained to catch the sound of anybody approaching.

Megan looked at her watch. "We're supposed to be back at the bus by now. Maybe they'll send out a search party for us?"

"Maybe they'll leave without us," said Samuel.

"Don't be stupid, why would they do that?" asked Pax.

Samuel stopped and squared up to Pax. "Who you calling stupid?"

Megan pulled them apart. "Stop it, you two. We're in enough trouble without the pair of you squabbling."

Pax was about to say it was Samuel's fault when a voice called out from the fog. Instinctively, Pax crouched low to the ground and fell silent, looking towards the noise. He felt sure the Pinchers would hear his heart beating like a drum inside his chest. He jumped when a little brown bird flitted down next to him, pecked at a tiny grub and then flew away.

The voice came again. Clearer this time, closer. What had the person called out? It sounded like Chin or Zin.

Chen started walking towards the voice and called out. "Ye ye?"

"What are you doing?" hissed Briony.

"Everyone, keep quiet," said Pax.

But Chen kept walking away from the others, shouting louder. "Ye ye, is that you?"

"Come back," said Samuel through gritted teeth.

A voice replied, but it was too faint to hear properly. It didn't sound English. Was the person speaking to Chen? She was half Chinese. Maybe they were conversing in Mandarin. But why was she walking towards a Pincher? Did she share Pax's view about them? He ran towards her but another bank of fog drifted across the path and swallowed her.

Pax turned to look at the others, who were still frozen to the spot. He didn't know what to do. He ran back.

"We need to get back to the bus," said Briony, looking at the time.

"Why did she go off like that?" said Megan. "When there are Pinchers around?"

"It sounded like she recognised the voice. How is that possible?" asked Samuel.

Pax shrugged. "I don't know. But we can't abandon her. Come on, let's form a line. All walk in the direction we last saw her. And make sure you keep an eye on whoever is next to you in the line. Roacher, you stay with us."

The four friends walked slowly forward, glancing left and right. After a few minutes there was nothing.

"We have to stop and get back to the bus, Pax," said Megan

Pax didn't want to give up yet. "But…"

"If we don't go now, the bus will leave without us. They'll assume we've all been captured. We'll never make it back to the Gate on our own."

"Megan's right," said Samuel.

Pax looked along the line and saw Briony nodding her head too. He felt sick. "OK. Roacher, show us the way back. No creeping along this time. Fast as you can."

Pax was very glad he'd decided to bring his little helper along. If it hadn't been for the guilt weighing down on his shoulders, he might have been proud of how well Roacher was doing. As the little rotor blades sped up, the buzz changed pitch from bumble bee to mosquito. They had to break into a gentle jog to keep up with the robot. Pax saw a tree and gate that looked familiar. "I think we're getting close now."

Another sound pierced the fog, straight ahead of them. Not a voice this time, but a mechanical noise. Pax stopped to listen. It sounded like the bus doors opening. Or closing. And then he heard the whine of the hover engines kicking into life.

"Quick! It's leaving without us!" he shouted.

"Not if I can help it," said Megan, sprinting ahead and disappearing into the fog.

Now there were only three of them. They were running too, guided by the sound of the engines but then that sound stopped, Pax's heart sank. Had the Pinchers captured the bus too? He had been teased all week for being worried about this trip. But it was true. This was the most dangerous thing they'd ever done. Maybe they'd never get back to the safety of The Wall.

A person was approaching through the fog. Pax slowed his run, wishing Roacher had some form of weapon. But all they had to defend themselves were a bunch of slightly pointed carrots.

His muscles tensed and then relaxed when he saw it was Megan, coming back with a smile on her face.

"I caught up with the bus. Hurry, they're all waiting for you."

They resumed their jog as Briony sniffed back tears. Pax's legs suddenly felt light and fresh again, knowing their ordeal was almost over. He told Roacher to climb back into his pocket. "Don't tell the others about my robot, OK, Briony?"

She nodded as the bus appeared through the fog. Back on board, Pax had to explain to the teacher how Chen had gone missing in the fog as they made their way to the Western Gate. It felt awful, like admitting he'd forgotten to do his homework, only a hundred times worse.

"Can't we go look for her in the bus?" Pax pleaded.

"No," said Sir Gawain. "My priority is to keep the rest of you safe. The other groups had their drones attacked too. The Defence League has been informed and a search team has been dispatched. You've done everything you could, Forby."

"What did they want, sir? Why did they pick on Chen?" asked Samuel.

"Who knows? Pinchers are very unpredictable."

[-]

The bus stopped outside the Western Gate and Pax could hear the driver speaking to the guards over a radio. As the gates cracked open, and the outskirts of New London became visible, there was a cheer from the other pupils. But Pax didn't feel like celebrating. He looked back towards the fog, thinking of Chen somewhere out there. Once the vehicle had passed through the gate it stopped next to one of its towers and everybody was asked to disembark.

After they had filed into an entrance hall at the base of the tower, Sir Gawain explained what was happening. "Standard procedure after spending time outside the Wall. Everyone has to pass through a scanner to make sure they've not picked up anything nasty."

Was it Pax's imagination, or did the teacher stare right at him when he said that last sentence? Pax's stomach knotted tight as he thought of Roacher, hiding in his pocket. It was too late to leave the little robot on the bus. Surely, he would be confiscated if they found him. Pax gritted his teeth. He couldn't bear to lose two friends on the same day!

The students lined up to go through the scanner. Pax positioned himself near the back of the queue to give himself some thinking time. One by one the children shuffled forwards, while Pax rubbed the back of his head and tried desperately to think of something. Each time a pupil passed through the rectangular frame of metal, a light above the frame flashed green, the machine beeped and the guard waved the pupil on, calling for the next person.

The sentry looked bored and tired. Perhaps that was Pax's best chance. As he approached the front of the queue, breathing hard, heart pounding, he bent down to adjust the laces on his boots. He lifted Roacher out of his pocket and placed him on the ground. "See you on the other side," he whispered.

Pax stood up and walked through the scanner. The beep and green light confirmed he was OK to proceed. Once through he pretended to stumble and as he put his hand down to the ground, Roacher scurried back into his hand. Pax stood up and carefully placed the little robot in his pocket. He breathed out with relief but as he stood, he locked eyes with Zachariah.

Pax froze, his heart in an ice-cold vice-like grip. Of all the people to have noticed, it just had to be him, didn't it? The tall boy raised his eyebrows as his lips creased into a wicked grin.

CHAPTER TWENTY-SEVEN

The bus arrived back at school and everyone was given a mug of hot chocolate as they traipsed into the building. Pax had spent the whole journey curled into a ball on his seat, worrying about Chen and wondering when Zachariah was going to tell Sir Gawain about Roacher. Pax was sure his little friend would cost the Judges some points, points they could ill afford to lose. Maybe he would get expelled straight away, or worse, have Roacher confiscated. He couldn't bear the thought of being parted.

But Zachariah didn't talk to the teacher on the hover-bus. He must have seen the robot. Why was he waiting? Pax did not believe for one minute the bully was being kind. Perhaps he was planning something worse. Whatever it was, Pax was desperate to get back to the dormitory and hide Roacher in his secret compartment. At least he could deny Zachariah's story then if the bully did tell.

But the first years were not allowed back to their rooms, not straight away. Pax could see the pings of chatter about Chen on his wrist tab as the story trended on Hansard. Pax, Samuel, Megan and Briony were asked to follow Sir Gawain to Miss Adams' office. A faint flicker of hope glowed in the darkness of Pax's thoughts. Maybe Miss Adams was back, at last?

They entered the office and Pax's heart sank immediately when he saw a stranger sitting behind the wide, teak desk. This was going to be the moment when Roacher was confiscated, he was sure of it. The woman beckoned for the friends to sit down.

Sir Gawain wheeled around to stand next to her. "This is Detective Inspector Braille from Scotland Yard. She will be running the investigation into Chen's disappearance. She has some questions for you. Just answer as best you can, OK?"

Pax let out a sigh of relief – this was nothing to do with Roacher – but realised that might look wrong, so tried to mask the noise with a sniff of his nose and a sad shake of his head.

The detective clasped her hands together on the desk and leant forward. "Och, this must be very upsetting for you poor dears. But I do need to know everything you can remember. What exactly happened out there?"

The friends shuffled in their chairs and when nobody else spoke up, Pax began to relate the events in the mist.

"So, you say the drone was shot down?" asked D.I. Braille, turning to Samuel.

He nodded. "First they took out the camera and then they fried the drone."

"Aye, that fits the pattern," she said.

"Have they done this before, then?" asked Pax.

"The Inspector is asking the questions, Forby," said Sir Gawain.

"It's alright," she said. She looked at her notes. "It's Pax, isn't it? Yes, Defence League patrols have been attacked before. Every time, the Pinchers go for the drones first. But this is the first time they have come near Osterley Farm. They must be getting bolder. OK, so after the drone crashed what happened?"

Pax continued the story in a juddering voice that he didn't have to fake this time. With every sentence, he wondered what they could have done differently, guilt stabbing him in the guts.

The inspector interrupted when it got to the part with the voice in the fog. "It was a drab day for sure. Can you remember exactly what that voice said?"

"Chin," said Pax.

"I thought it sounded more like Zin," said Megan.

The inspector scribbled something down in her note book. "Most likely it was Chen's name, but spoken in her native tongue." She repeated the name, moving her lips in an odd fashion.

"Yes, that was it," said Pax. "And she said: is that you ye-ye?"

"Ye-ye?" repeated the detective.

Pax nodded while D.I. Braille noted something else down.

"Then she just disappeared into the fog," said Pax. "We tried to find her, but she was…we couldn't…" He shook his head. "So, we went to find the bus."

"Thank you, children. You've been very helpful. That will be all," said the Inspector.

"Alright, you can go back to your common room now," said Sir Gawain.

As they stood up to leave, Megan said, "What does it mean? Ye-ye? Is it a mandarin word?"

Ms Braille nodded. "It means Grandpa."

"One of the Pinchers was her Grandpa? Why would he want to kidnap her?" asked Pax.

"Chances are, it was just a wee trick to lure her away. Poor child."

Pax locked away his guilt about Chen and ran the whole way back to the Judges' common room, desperate to hide Roacher before Zachariah squealed. Samuel entered the dormitory just as Pax was closing his secret drawer.

"I'm sure Zachariah saw Roacher back at the gate," said Pax. "I don't know why he hasn't snitched yet but I've got to keep him hidden for a while."

"That would've really capped things off today if Roacher had been confiscated." Samuel looked down at the ground and put his hands in his pockets. "Pax, about your stone…"

"You don't have to explain, Samuel." Pax felt too wrung about by the day's emotions to argue about the glow stone now. But he couldn't hide the disappointment, so his voice had a hard edge to it. "If you didn't like my present, you could've just said. I'd have given it to Megan, or something."

"What? Mate, I loved it. It's just that… over Christmas, me dad was in a bad way. Depression, the doc' said. Why do people get depressed at Christmas? Supposed to be a happy time, in'it?"

"Sorry to hear that." Pax's frosty stance towards his room-mate began to melt.

"When I showed me dad your present his face lit up like a Christmas tree. Thought it was bloomin' awesome. So, I gave it to him. Sorry."

Pax's heart lifted a little, pleased that Samuel's dad liked the glow-stone. His stomach fizzed with guilt for doubting his friend before he knew the facts. Finally, he smiled at his roommate, happy that they weren't falling out again. As the mix of emotions swirled around his body, Pax suddenly felt very tired. He slumped down on the bed and curled up, falling asleep in his outdoor clothes, on top of the duvet.

[-]

For the next few days, Pax could tell that the rest of the school was talking about the incident at the farm. Whenever he walked past, pupils stopped their conversations and just stared at him. There were no further interviews with the Inspector. Pax asked Sir Gawain if there had been any progress but was just told 'enquiries were ongoing.'

Pax knew it was hopeless really. There was nothing to go on. Even if the Defence League sent half their squads out beyond The Wall, they wouldn't know where to look. He tried to keep his spirits up by telling himself that Chen had recognised that voice in the mist. Maybe it really had been her Grandad after all. Without any parents, perhaps she was happy to be re-united with him, somewhere out in the countryside.

"Cheer up," said Samuel one evening. "Global chess tournament is coming up next week. Sukhwinder tells me you're really good now. Must have a chance of winning that for the Judges. We could do with the points."

The tournament, of course! Pax had been so distracted by Chen's disappearance that he'd not kept up his practice. "I'm a bit rusty. Let's have a game."

"Not much practice playing me, I'm useless at this."

Megan shook her head. "Me too."

Briony had just walked into the common room. She wandered over to join them. "Useless at what?"

"I need a playing partner to practise against," said Pax, pointing at the board.

"Oh, I played quite a bit in junior school. I'll give you a game."

As they set up the board, Samuel whispered to Pax. "Stop grinning like a maniac. You'll scare her off."

Pax was tempted not to try too hard, so that the game would last a bit longer. But he soon realised Briony was a very good player, much better than Sukhwinder. Pax would have to play his best if he wanted to win. It was just so hard to concentrate, sitting opposite the prettiest girl in the school.

CHAPTER TWENTY-EIGHT

T he clouds and fog vanished one morning as though someone had ripped away London's duvet, leaving the city cold and exposed. Sunlight streamed in through the stone-framed windows that looked east across the Thames. The bare trees on the far bank were silvered with frost and the people out walking were plumped up with extra layers of clothing. With the shock of Chen's disappearance fading, the school returned to normal life, even though Pax was still having trouble sleeping. Every time he closed his eyes, he saw the girl fading into a bank of fog.

Pax yawned as he sat down in the canteen next to Samuel. Lumpy porridge for breakfast and it was so cold outside the pupils didn't even complain. Homework resumed for the first years and cleaning duties continued for the Judges.

After the day's lessons, Pax and Megan were sweeping the vast expanse of Westminster Hall. The hard work was, at least, keeping them warm. They started at the far end, near the newly glazed window.

"That's where he crashed through, isn't it?" said Pax.

Megan looked up. "Who? Oh, him. The Talks Party protester. I wonder what happened to him? I never read about any trial."

"And where is Miss Adams? She can't *still* be recovering, surely, just from a bump on the head?"

"My ma says they can be nasty things. You never quite know what's going on inside somebody's skull."

"Something's not right. I have a funny feeling," said Pax.

"That'll be the pigeon pie we had for lunch." Megan gave a chuckle at her own joke.

"I'm serious." Pax rested his broom against his chest as he counted items on his fingers. "The mayor has outlawed The Talks

Party, branding them terrorists, even though they want peace. And now Miss Adams is out of the way, all of our recent lessons seem to be about war and fighting. We wouldn't have had to go out to Osterley Farm if the third years weren't doing some Defence League exercise."

Megan shrugged. "What can we do about it?"

"If we could get Miss Adams back, I'm sure lessons would return to normal. I'm going to find out where she is."

"How?" asked Samuel.

"I asked Miss Bowie about the Headmistress earlier today. She wouldn't say anything specific but I have a feeling Miss Adams is being looked after here on site. The teacher said there was no news *from the nurse*. Not from the hospital, or from the doctors. From the nurse. And we never did see an Ambulance drone come to pick her up that day. I'm going to send Roacher to check out the infirmary tonight."

"I thought you were keeping him hidden from Zachariah?" Megan whispered.

"I can't keep him locked away forever. Besides, that numbskull seems to have forgotten all about it. Come on, let's get this sweeping done before we miss supper."

[-]

The little window high up the wall of the dormitory was clouded over with condensation as the sky finally began to lose its darkness. Pax hugged his knees to his chest, eyes fixed on the doorway into their room. He didn't even notice Samuel wake up.

"You look terrible, mate. You been up all night with Roacher?"

Pax shook his head. "He never came back."

"He'll be along soon. Come on, let's get dressed for breakfast. Wouldn't want to miss lumpy porridge, would yer?"

Pax tried to smile but he couldn't help worrying. He didn't remember getting dressed but, somehow, he ended up in the canteen eating breakfast with Samuel and Megan. Samuel whispered the news about Roacher to Megan.

"Why don't you ask Briony for another game of global chess?" asked Megan. "She said she really enjoyed the last game."

143

"Oooh," said Samuel, fluttering his eyelids and making silly kissing noises. "Please Pax, you're so wonderful at chess."

"Not today, guys." Pax stood up and cleared away his untouched breakfast. He crept into one of the boiler rooms in the basement and leant his head against the heat until he was dripping with sweat. Then he hurried to the infirmary wing, hoping to be admitted.

"Can I help you, Pax Forby?" asked the medical robot on reception.

Pax groaned. "I'm not feeling very well."

The droid's face monitor blinked. "What sort of not-very-well?"

"A bit feverish."

The metal nurse shone a beam at Pax's forehead. "Body temperature is elevated and heart rate is a little high. I suggest plenty of bedrest. I will issue a notice to your teachers today."

Before Pax could reply, he heard a beep and the whooshing sound of electronic mail being posted. "Thanks," he muttered. Not bedrest! He wanted to be let into the infirmary. But Pax was never any good at making things up on the spot. He couldn't think of anything else to say, so he just returned to his room. He thought it was a bit odd that the nurse was so quick to sign him off from lessons for the day. If the other pupils knew that, they'd be queuing up right down the corridor.

Just as he got back to his room, his wrist tab buzzed. A video message had arrived. Pax tapped the screen to start playing the message and recoiled at the sight of Zachariah's grinning face.

"Look who's come to visit the Loyals, Pax." He stepped back from the camera which zoomed in on the desk behind Zachariah. The picture was fuzzy at first. When it re-focused, Pax gasped. Roacher was tied up, lying on his back with wires wrapped around its little metal body. Two legs had squirmed free and were scrabbling in the air as if the robot were waving for help. "And you thought I'd forgotten all about your little pet, hadn't you? Don't worry, it's perfectly safe. For now."

Pax pressed the pause button and punched his pillow a dozen times. "No! No! No!" He ground his teeth and wiped at his eyes before watching the rest of the video.

"I intend to win next week's chess tournament," said Zachariah. "I hear that you're on the Judges' team and that you're pretty good. So, here's the deal. You can win some group stage games but if you end up playing me, you make sure you lose, OK? If you do that, I'll let you have this machine back. If not, well, let's just say I'll introduce your robot to my friend, Mr Hammer. I'm sure they'll have a smashing time together."

Pax pulled the wrist tab off and hurled it across the room.

CHAPTER TWENTY-NINE

After supper, Pax and his friends went to sit in front of the fire in the Judges' common room. It had been eel pie, followed by apple crumble.

"Oh man, that was so good," said Samuel with a groan as he lay back on a sofa.

"Too much crumble, too much crumble," said Megan patting her stomach.

Pax waited until the friends were out of earshot of others in the common room. They sat up sharply when he explained about his video message from Zachariah.

"Why does he keep picking on you? And why does he have to win at everything?" asked Briony.

"He was like that in junior school," said Samuel. "So competitive. Heard his dad tellin' my mum how his precious son was going to be star pupil when he graduated."

"What's that?" asked Pax.

"You know how graduates from the winning party get the best jobs when they leave? Well, the *star* pupil from the winning party gets a spot on the Council," replied Megan.

"Cor, can you imagine someone like that helping the mayor run the city?" said Samuel with a roll of his eyes.

Pax didn't care about the Council. He just wanted to be an Engineer. And to get his little metal friend back.

"Why don't you tell the teachers what's he done?" said Briony.

Pax shook his head. "Can't do that. They don't even know Roacher exists."

"But why? If I were clever enough to build something like that, I'd want everyone to know," she replied.

"Artificial intelligences are strictly forbidden," said Samuel.

"So, what you gonna do?" asked Megan.

"Briony can win the tournament for us instead," said Pax. "Win it for Chen."

Everybody was silent for a moment as they thought of the missing girl.

It was Briony's turn to shake her head. "I'm not sure I'm good enough to do that." She looked around the room to see who else was in earshot. "And the other Judges in the tournament aren't great either. I watched them practice the other day."

Each year the Global Chess tournament consisted of 24 players. From each of the four Parties, there were six representatives. A boy and a girl from each of the three years. Pax and Briony would be the first-year players for the Judges this time. Obviously, Zachariah would be one of the first years for the Loyals.

"We could do with the points," said Megan. "Judges are still last, and I don't fancy cleaning duties for another term while trying to revise for exams."

Pax didn't care about cleaning duties but the threat of expulsion at year-end was looming over him. He felt like he was being torn apart, pulled in different directions by a pair of squabbling giants. Chess had been his one chance to help the Judges catch up the other parties. But he couldn't abandon Roacher, not after all this time. It was so maddening! And so unfair. He realised he was almost yanking the arms off his chair and the others were all staring at him. Pax gently uncurled his fingers from the armrests and tried to slow his breathing. "I'm going to bed."

[-]

Straight after breakfast, Pax headed back to the infirmary and complained about the same illness as yesterday after spending time heating up in the boiler room. The medical droid signed him off from lessons again. Just what Pax needed. He went to the engineering lab and checked the timetable. There wouldn't be a class in here until mid-morning. He let himself in, too busy to worry about being caught and started shaping some spare bits of metal into a familiar form. He rooted around in a box of tiny robot pieces and found six near-identical legs. He just managed to fix them onto the strange figure before Sir Brunor wheeled into the laboratory.

"What are you doing in here, boy?" asked the teacher.

Pax quickly pocketed his little machine. "Err... Err... Just doing some extra practice, sir. Trying to revise as I go along. All these new lessons about guns and tanks, there's a lot to take in."

Sir Brunor's emoji face pursed its lips and blinked. "Hmm, well get along now. I have a class to teach."

Pax gave himself a little pat on the back as he left. He'd managed to make up an excuse, on the spot. On his way back to the dormitory, he made a stop at the cupboard where the maintenance staff kept spare parts for the robot teachers and wiring for the school system. The cupboard was locked, but with everybody else in lessons, he used his lockpick. After a couple of panicked failures, the lock finally opened with a satisfying click. He found the items he needed and sprinted back to his bedroom.

Samuel walked in as Pax was attaching a head and antennae to the metal body. "How come you missed lessons all morning?"

"I told nurse I had a bug."

"If only that were true." Samuel peered at the thing Pax was holding. "Wait, is that a new Roacher?"

"I can't replace him like a worn-out toy," said Pax.

"No, course not. I just wondered..."

Pax sighed. "A back-up plan, in case Briony can't win."

"You look tired. You should get some rest this afternoon," said Samuel.

[-]

The fire alarm went off at two o'clock in the morning. Earlier that evening, as the friends had cleaned up in the kitchen, Pax had stuffed a toaster with some paper and used a timer plug to switch it on just before 2am. His back-up plan for the chess tournament wouldn't work if the others knew about it.

Everybody shuffled out of school, looking shocked, angry or half-asleep, with either their duvet wrapped round their shoulders or wearing a coat over their pyjamas. Pax stooped to tie his boot laces, separating him from Samuel. When nobody was looking, he ducked into a darkened alcove and watched the rest of the school file past.

Watching through a window as the pupils lumbered out through the porch of Victoria Tower and into the gardens beyond, Pax saw flakes of snow begin to fall for the first time that winter.

Pax donned his goggles and hoodie and ran off to complete his mission. Twenty minutes later he was waiting near the porch as the others traipsed back inside.

"Mate, that was wicked wursh," said Samuel as he spotted Pax just ahead of him in the corridor.

Pax turned to look at his friend. "What was?"

"The snowball fight, dummy. Didn't you join in?" Samuel looked at Pax's coat and pyjamas which was dry as a bone. "Come to think of it, I didn't even see you outside."

"Where else would I have been?"

CHAPTER THIRTY

The chess players gathered in the Long Gallery after breakfast, as well as a small group of spectators. Most pupils were yawning following their disturbed night and some of the third-year players were nursing cups of coffee. Pax could see the steam rising from their mugs. The smell caught in the back of his throat, like burnt toffee or roast chestnuts. He didn't normally like coffee, but that morning the aroma was almost irresistible.

Sir Galahad wheeled up the aisle between the rows of Global Chess boards. He turned to face the contestants and waited for silence. "Now, you should all know the rules. Each game will last no more than an hour. If there is no decisive winner by then, the board computer will determine which player has the advantage. During a game, there is to be no conferring with other players or spectators. We will play the first three rounds of group games this morning and then finish off the group stages after lunch. The screen behind me shows which table you are on for your first game, so take your places. And remember, New London is no place for losers!"

"We will win," mumbled the players and spectators.

Pax gave a nervous smile to Briony and walked to his table, rubbing the metal dots on the back of his head. He'd only ever played against Megan, Sukhwinder and Briony. Was he good enough to beat players from other parties with their own favourite tactics? At least the draw had been kind, he'd avoided Zachariah's group.

A second-year boy from Chancellors was already waiting for him. Pax got to choose Empires first and selected Asia, while the other boy picked America. Pax was too cautious with his first few moves. But he soon realised that the Chancellor boy was not that good. He attacked too soon, before he had built up a proper army and Pax's submarines smashed the American navy. Once Pax's trade links with Africa were established, the money began to roll in and in a few turns his army was twice the size of the American forces. Invading through Alaska, he conquered the other player's capital well before the hour was up.

He stood up to shake hands and noticed the other boy blushing. None of the other games had finished yet. Pax breathed a sigh of relief, happy to get an easy first win under his belt. He looked up at the big screen showing progress in all of the other games. Briony was doing well against another first year from Peers but unfortunately Zachariah was about to beat the third-year girl from Judges.

Two of the games continued through to the end of the hour. When Sir Galahad announced the end of play a hush descended on the room as players and spectators waited to see who the computer would declare to have the edge. In Pax's group a third-year girl from Peers was victorious, while in Briony's group a second-year Loyal refused to accept that he was behind. Sir Galahad went over to the table and pointed out the weakness in the Loyal player's trade links and the other player's dominance of the North Pole.

"The computer is always right, Jenkins. Any more protests and I'll have you disqualified."

While the scores were recorded – a player received three points for a win, two for an advantage and one point for merely not losing – Pax grabbed a drink and slurped at it contentedly. He saw Briony, next to the spectators' seating, chatting to Megan.

"Well done," he said. "Always good to start off with a win." After all their practice together, Pax found his tongue had finally loosened up when he talked with Briony.

"You too. Looks like you've got a tough match next."

"Yep. Tamsin Smith. Captain of the Peer's team and last year's winner."

"Good luck," said Megan.

"I'll need it," said Pax biting his nails.

Tamsin chose to play Europe, which meant Pax could stick with his favourite Asian empire. It was much tougher than the previous game, with both players building up good defences and trade routes at first, leaving the aggressive tactics for later. After forty-five minutes there was nothing in it. Pax's head was throbbing as Tamsin tried to conquer his trading posts in Africa. Pax just managed to beat off the attack and was building up a navy to invade South America when Sir Galahad declared that the hour was up.

Pax wiped sweaty hands on his trousers as he stood to shake with Tamsin. He wasn't sure if he'd done enough, and she was probably his biggest threat to winning this group. Looking up at the score board, Pax could see that Briony had won her second match easily. And Zachariah's game had also lasted the full hour. The tall Loyals' boy ran his fingers through his hair and his lips were pulled tight.

The computer on Pax's board declared that he had the advantage. He clenched his fist in delight.

"You were lucky," said Tamsin with a shake of her head.

He was about to say something about sore losers, when the computer on Zachariah's table declared that his opponent had edged past. "Yes!" shouted Pax, causing everyone to turn and stare at him. Pax didn't care. Maybe the bully wouldn't win his group and Pax wouldn't have to lose to him after all. Zachariah kicked the table leg and stomped over to get a drink.

In the third round of games, Pax just managed to beat Helen, a fellow Judge in the second year. Briony and Zachariah's games went on for the full hour and the computers declared that both players had the advantage. It was time for lunch. Pax's head was sore and his stomach rumbled as he made his way to the canteen.

"See," said Megan as the four friends sat down together for some pasta, "I told you. You can do this."

"Both of you, top of your groups. Very nice," said Samuel.

"Thanks," said Briony. "And even better, Zachariah was edged out in one of his games."

Pax shook his head. "He still got a point. Group C looks really tight. I wouldn't count him out yet." He picked at his food, with little appetite.

[-]

After lunch, doubt began to nibble away at Pax's confidence, like waves eating away at a crumbling cliff. Zachariah won again and would top his group if he could beat his last opponent, a third-year from Peers who was runner-up last year. Pax won his fourth game easily, but Briony had a close match with a second-year Loyal. Pax could tell from the board that she was in trouble, so he went over to stand next to her. She looked close to tears when the computer declared that the Loyal boy had edged it.

Pax gave her hand a squeeze. "You can still win your group. Play defensively in your last match. As long as you get a point, you're through to the semi-finals."

In the final round of group games, Pax kept looking across at Briony's match and up at the big screen to see how she was getting on. He was pretty sure he'd won his group already. With his tiredness and the distraction of Briony's game, his match went the full hour and Pax ended up being edged out. He still won Group A with eleven points, ahead of Tamsin with nine but chided himself for not concentrating. He couldn't afford any more slip-ups.

Briony had followed Pax's advice and didn't attack once during the entire game. Her opponent was given the advantage, but she'd earned a point and with it she won group B by the narrowest of margins. "Thank you", she whispered to Pax as she got up from her board. Pax's heart grew so big, he felt sure it would burst from his chest.

In group C, Zachariah's game had lasted the full hour too and he needed the edge to get through to the semi-finals. Pax and Briony stood shoulder to shoulder as they waited for the result. Their knees sagged as the computer declared Zachariah had the advantage and won the group.

The tall boy punched the air and turned his hands into pistols, aiming shots at the two first years from the Judges' party. "I'm a-coming for ya," he said in a phoney American accent. He would be Briony's opponent in one of the semi-finals.

Pax stifled a groan and pulled Briony away. "Come on, there's a half-hour break before the semi-finals. Let's get some fresh air."

They went up some spiral stairs in the corner of Victoria Tower and kept climbing past the library entrance until they reached the roof. The Guild of Cities' green standard with its silver cog wheel and spanner fluttered in the cold breeze on top of the huge flagpole. The days were getting longer, but the wind still had fangs of winter. Neither of them wore coats. Their eyes watered from the breeze and they huddled close for warmth. As Briony leaned into him, Pax curled his arm around her shoulder as if it was the most natural thing in the world to do.

"So, you reckon we can get an all-Judges final?" she asked.

Pax tried to shrug without letting go. He was freezing cold but he would have happily stayed like that all afternoon. "I'm sure you can beat Zachariah, but I've got that third-year Loyal girl. She won group D easily."

Briony turned to face Pax with a smile. "You'll be fine." She started to go back inside, but halfway to the door she stopped. Returning to Pax's side she took his hand and gave him a peck on the cheek. "Good luck," she whispered.

Pax felt like his chest was going to explode. His heart was racing, his cheek felt hot where she'd kissed him and all his tiredness seemed to fall away as if he were a reptile that had shed its old, dry skin.

CHAPTER THIRTY-ONE

Back in the Long Gallery, the audience of pupils had doubled in size. All of the Peers and Chancellors groaned when they saw that none of their players had made it to the semi-finals, while the group of spectators from the Judges and Loyals were cheering loudly. The noise and the glare of hundreds of eyes pressed down on Pax, but he was still feeling the glow from that wonderful moment at the top of Victoria Tower. Right now, he reckoned he could take on the whole school.

Sir Galahad soon put a stop to the noise. "Silence, please. We are about to start the semi-finals. On the first table, we have Pax Forby representing the Judges against Hayley Robertson for the Loyals." Both groups of spectators whooped as their player's name was read out. "And on the second table, Briony Latimer against Zachariah Thomson, also Judges versus Loyals. Players, please take your places."

Hayley won the toss and chose the empire that Pax preferred to play – Asia – but even that couldn't dampen Pax's spirits. He was fully focused. The board seemed to come alive in his mind's eye, with ships crashing through towering waves, tanks rolling over muddy plains while planes streaked overhead. The battle for world supremacy began.

Pax quickly figured out Hayley's tactics. He could see her next move in his mind. He laid traps with his submarines for her fleet. He pretended to play defensively at first, then launched a devastating attack on Siberia and used it as a stepping stone to harass the Chinese capital. In what seemed like no time at all, Hayley stood up and offered Pax her hand as he swept to victory. The Judges cheered and shouted his name. Whatever happened in the final, he was finally going to get some points. The relief washed over him like a warm summer breeze.

As Pax waved to his supporters, he realised that the other game was far from over. His own game had lasted longer than he realised and the sixty minutes were nearly up. Pax edged towards Briony's table and watched as the other semi-final played out its last few moves. He could tell that neither side was going to win in time, so Pax was carefully noting the position of the pieces and the regions each side controlled. It was going to be close, but Zachariah's last move had put him in a strong position. If Briony didn't react now it would be too late. Pax's heart squeezed tight.

He watched Briony ponder over her last move. She was staring at the wrong part of the globe. She needed to attack South America! Pax was desperate to tell her. He bit his bottom lip, trying to keep the words from blurting out. He knew that if he gave her any advice, Sir Galahad would make her forfeit the game and he might even disqualify Pax from the final, giving Zachariah victory by default.

Pax balled his fists tight and shoved them into his pockets. As the seconds ticked down and Briony made the wrong attack, Pax's fingernails dug into the palms of his hands.

The hour was over. Pax tried to smile at Briony as she rose from her seat. The Loyals knew their man had done it and were singing his name even before the computer confirmed the result. Zachariah had made it to the final. He turned to look at Pax with a grin and taking careful aim with his finger pistol, he pulled the trigger and blew smoke from the pretend barrel. Pax felt a stabbing pain in his chest as if the bullet had been real.

"Well done to both boys. I'm sure the final will be a great contest. We'll start again in half an hour, after everybody's had a chance for some tea," said Sir Galahad.

[-]

They tried to console Briony as they ate a quick meal in the canteen. The dining hall was filled with excited chatter. Pax got a few slaps on the back from other Judges. But Zachariah got some

156

good-lucks from Peers and Chancellors who really didn't want the Judges to catch up in the Polls.

Briony was almost in tears and hardly touched her food. "I'm so sorry, Pax. I messed everything up."

Pax tried to smile. "Not at all. You played really well. That semi-final could have gone either way."

"But now you'll have to lose on purpose," said Megan. "Zachariah's already a smug git. And he's going to be even worse after this."

"Not to mention the Polls," said Samuel, looking at the board. "Points for coming second won't be enough for us to catch Peers and Chancellors." It was 20 points for the winner and only 5 for being runner-up.

LOYALS	168
CHANCELLORS	145
PEERS	141
JUDGES	123

Pax sighed. "Thanks for reminding me."

"You couldn't, you know, build another Roacher and play to win, could you?"

"You don't get it. Roacher isn't just a machine. He's... He's family." Pax's eyes began to well up. And he could tell Zachariah was watching from across the room with his group of adoring friends. Pax wasn't going to give them the satisfaction of seeing him upset so he scooped up the remainder of his meal and cleared it away before going back to his dormitory.

[-]

When Pax returned to the Long Gallery it felt like the whole school had turned out to watch. Sir Galahad had to link his voice into the school speaker system to get himself heard as he announced the start of the Grand Final, the best of three games. Pax won the toss and chose Asia. He set up his pieces and played out the first few moves as normal and then began to make small

157

but deliberate mistakes. It left a horrible taste in his mouth. His hand almost refused to co-operate as his heart screamed in protest. A city left undefended. A fleet of tankers sent across an ocean where Zachariah's submarines lurked.

Even though he couldn't see him, Pax just knew his opponent would be grinning on the other side of the globe. And that just made the lump of dread in his stomach grow even larger. After only half an hour, the first game was over. A clear win for the Loyals. As the two boys stood up, Zachariah whispered to Pax. "That's a good boy. One more win and I'll release your precious little robot."

Pax ground his teeth together, forcing out quiet words. "You'd better."

All the Loyal supporters cheered like mad as the scoreboard ticked over to show Zachariah three-nil up, but the rest of the crowd groaned at the quick and unexpected loss for the Judges' player. Someone booed and another person yelled out. "What's the matter, Forby? He paid you off?"

Pax looked up sharply but couldn't see where the accusation had come from. Was it that obvious he was losing on purpose?

In the next game, Zachariah chose to be Asia and Pax was Europe. In the first few moves, Pax was passive but sensible, building up a strong merchant fleet and opening trade links with America. He could tell that Zachariah was being sloppy in his play, counting on the fact that Pax would soon throw the game on purpose.

But after half an hour, Pax had made no mistakes and Zachariah's early errors were beginning to compound on themselves. He kicked at the table legs, making the globe wobble and he stabbed at the keyboard each time he made an increasingly frantic move. But the more desperately Zachariah tried, the easier it became for Pax to stay ahead without even attacking the Asians. At the end of the hour, the computer declared that Pax had the advantage. The cheers were almost deafening. The scoreboard changed to show a two-one win for Pax, but with Zachariah still ahead overall 4-2.

"What do you think you're doing?" said the bully in a low voice as they moved away from the table for a quick break.

Pax just shrugged. "Got to make it look close, haven't we? Besides, unless I thrash you in the last game, you've still got enough points to win the trophy."

While Pax gulped down a mug of hot chocolate, he could hear his friends shouting out his name. He refused to look across, but instead just stared into his drink, focusing on what he had to do. Zachariah had gone to the loo and when he came back, his grin returned with him. Pax could see he was clutching something in his hand. With a lurch of his stomach, Pax realised what it was. Roacher, tied up and covered in a little cloth bag with just a single, bent antennae sticking out.

As they sat down for the final game, Zachariah whispered again. "Just in case you've forgotten our little arrangement, Forby. You lose this last game or I squash your bug flat. Right here, in front of you."

Pax was shaking as he took his place in front of the globe. He gripped the edge of the table so hard his knuckles turned white.

"Everything alright, Forby?" asked Sir Galahad, his emoji face assuming a kind expression of concern.

Pax breathed in slowly and puffed his chest out. "Yes, sir. Thank you. Everything's fine."

"Right, let's get on with it, shall we? Thomson's turn to choose sides. The deciding match!"

Zachariah began setting up his forces as the Americans, accompanied by more cheers from the spectators. Pax was glad he had his back to most of them. He needed to concentrate.

This time, Zachariah was playing hard from the off. He was obviously suspicious of Pax's tactics and wasn't taking anything for granted. Pax settled into the game with his usual early tactics as the Asian player, focusing on trade links and resources. After half an hour, neither player had made a single act of aggression. A draw would keep Zachariah ahead in the overall score. He had no need to attack. But what he didn't realise was that Pax had built up a hidden flotilla of submarines, not shown on the board, but stored in the computer's memory.

With fifteen minutes left, Pax began amassing an invasion force. He knew that Zachariah would react and start building up

159

his own submarines to blow the invading ships out of the water before they could land their troops. With ten minutes until the end of the hour, Pax held back his invasion force but instead sent all of his navy into the oceans controlled by Zachariah. There was a furious battle. Pax just about won but most of his ships and submarines were destroyed in the process. He looked up at the clock. Five minutes remaining. Would it be time enough?

Zachariah was rocking back in his chair, balancing on its rear legs. He had placed the bag that contained Roacher on the floor, right next to the table. Every time he sat forward, the front legs of the chair banged back down, just missing Roacher's bag.

Pax gulped. He looked across at the Judges who were cheering like mad, sensing that he might still be able to win a clear victory. He found Samuel, Megan and Briony in the sea of faces. The two girls were holding each other's arms, all nervous smiles. Samuel was grim-faced but when he saw Pax watching, he just nodded. Pax swallowed hard, sure of what he had to do.

He turned back to focus on the globe and launched a devastating invasion of Canada across the Arctic circle. He didn't need his navy for this. Zachariah had made a blunder, assuming the attack would come across the sea. He tried to amass enough defenders, but with two minutes left on the clock, Pax's tanks rolled into Washington. He had won a crushing victory. The scoreboard ticked over to show Pax now had five points, with Zachariah stuck on four. The crowd went absolutely crazy, the room shaking with noise.

As Pax stood up, Zachariah nudged Roacher's bag with his foot and brought the chair crashing down onto all four legs again. There was a horrible crunching sound as one of the legs of the chair landed right on top of the bag containing the little robot.

"Oops," said Zachariah.

CHAPTER THIRTY-TWO

gnoring the cheers and his pounding headache, Pax bent down and cupped his hands around the bag. He placed it carefully in his pocket, trying not to spill any pieces of the robot's shattered body. The spectators were cheering and waving their arms in the air. Sir Galahad was saying something to Pax. But everything was quiet and distant, as though Pax were watching the scene through a thick pane of glass.

The air seemed thick and his lungs heaved in effort. Pax waited while things happened around him before leaving the Gallery. He headed back to the Judges' common room, feeling oddly numb. Sitting in front of the fire, the heat slowly melted his numbness and the faint hint of a smile pulled at the corners of his mouth.

Megan ran into the room and threw her arms around him. "Oh Pax!"

"We're sorry about Roacher," said Briony, following the other girl into the common room.

Samuel waited for Megan's hug to end and patted his friend on the shoulder. "You toasted him at the end. That was really brave, mate."

"Look at the score," said Megan.

They all turned to see the Judges had edged ahead of Peers but the Loyals still had a decent lead over the rest.

LOYALS	173
CHANCELLORS	145
JUDGES	143
PEERS	141

"If I hadn't messed up my semi-final, we would have caught Chancellors too and Roacher would still be in one piece," said Briony with a shake of her head.

Pax stood up, the adrenaline of the match starting to fade, replaced with waves of fatigue and a hint of hope that he might not be expelled at the end of the year. "The main thing is we're not last anymore. Come on, I've got something to show you."

All around them, Judges were celebrating like mad and chanting songs about Pax the conquering hero. The four friends weaved through the crowd as Pax led them towards his and Samuel's dormitory.

On the stairs, Samuel asked "Are girls even allowed up here?"

Pax's head drooped and rocked from side to side. "Just for once, Samuel, let the rules slide, OK?"

"No-one's going to check right now," said Megan as she pushed past.

When they got to the room, Pax closed the door behind them and went over to his bedside table. He opened the secret compartment and pulled out something small. When he turned around and held out his hands, the others gasped. Roacher. In one piece, his slender antennae waggling from side to side and blue eyes peering out. The little robot beeped, dipped his legs then scurried up Pax's sleeve to his shoulder. Pax's face cracked into a huge grin.

"But. How did you?"

"Is that?"

"That can't be."

"I suppose I'd better explain," said Pax. "But first, and this is really important, you mustn't let anybody outside this room know."

The others ran forward and joined in a group hug. Pax tried to hold back tears. Encircled by his friends, he'd never felt happier.

"If Zachariah ever finds out I've tricked him, he's going to be furious. He's already mad for losing the final. No doubt he'll try to get his revenge somehow."

"He'll have to go through us first," said Megan, breaking off the hug.

"Yeah," said Samuel, smacking a fist against a palm.

"I told you Samuel, yesterday, that Roacher was irreplaceable. But that wasn't entirely true. I got enough parts to build a rough copy of him. No brain, not even any motors for movement, but it didn't need those. It just needed to look a bit like Roacher."

"So, what are you saying? You switched the fake Roacher for the real one, without him noticing? But how?" asked Megan.

"Remember the fire alarm last night? I set that off and hid while the school was evacuated. I figured I knew where Zachariah would be keeping Roacher, so I broke into the Loyal dormitories when everybody was outside having that snowball fight. And switched robots." Pax sat on the bed, smiling and pleased with himself.

"You droid-head!" said Samuel. "You could've told us. We were doing our nut during the final!"

"Not to mention upsetting me over the semis," said Briony, cuffing his shoulder.

"Don't you get it? I had to make it seem like we were all worried, otherwise Zachariah would've suspected something was up. If he'd checked what was in the bag, it would've been pretty obvious it wasn't the real thing. My whole plan rested on him not noticing. So, I wasn't faking it if I seemed nervous."

"That is brilliant," said Megan.

Pax looked at his friends. "You guys are brilliant. Come on, shall we join the party downstairs?"

[-]

Pax turned in for bed early. The chess tournament had been exhausting and the fire-alarm antics of the previous night meant that he could barely keep his eyes open as he hauled himself back upstairs to the dormitory. As he climbed into bed, Roacher beeped and crawled out from under the bed. Pax stroked his carapace and smiled. The little robot tickled Pax's ear with its antennae but Pax was already falling asleep. The last thing he saw before he closed his eyes was Roacher on top of the bed post, alert and watchful.

When Pax finally awoke the sun was casting patterns through the tiny window onto the floor of the dormitory. Roacher jumped up and down on Pax's chest and the boy ran his finger down the robot's metal body. The two of them played together until eventually their antics woke Samuel in the other bed.

"What time did you get to bed?" asked Pax.

Samuel rubbed his eyes and yawned. "I remember hot chocolate with marshmallows at midnight. Sometime after that, I suppose."

"What are we going to do today?" It was Sunday which meant no lessons.

"If it's snowed again, I'm going outside. But you've got two days of lessons to catch up on. You can borrow me notes if you want."

Those lies to the medical droid in the run-up to the chess tournament weighed down on Pax's shoulders. His smile quickly disappeared. Ugh. Samuel was right, of course. Even if he avoided expulsion, Pax couldn't fail his end-of-year exams if he wanted to be an engineer. But school work on a Sunday wasn't going to be easy with everyone else outside having fun in the snow.

[-]

Halfway through the morning Pax had caught up on several missed lessons. He turned to the next section of Samuel's notes and saw that it was programming and coding. Pax was way ahead of the rest of the class for this topic anyway, so he skipped this section and decided he'd earned himself a break. He went out to get a snack of whelk-flavoured crisps.

On his way back to the bedroom, Pax noticed some third years watching a film being projected onto the common room wall by cinebot. He didn't recognise the film, but it did trigger a memory – Roacher's mission the night he'd been kidnapped. Pax dashed back upstairs, and called for Roacher. The little robot scuttled into view. "Have you got some video footage to show me, little buggy?"

Roacher dipped his antennae and positioned himself on top of Pax's bedside drawers. Looking at the wall, Roacher beamed out a view of his ill-fated mission to find Miss Adams. Pax watched the jerky film as it showed Roacher's journey along the floors of the school, up the walls, squeezing through little gaps as the robot made its way towards the infirmary. The picture was the ghoulish green of a night-vision camera. Pax edged forward in his seat, praying for an answer to the mystery.

He watched the little robot visit three empty booths in the infirmary before crawling under a door into a more private room. Roacher scuttled up the frame of the bed and looked at the patient. A screen above the bed showed read-outs for heart rate, blood pressure and oxygen levels with some numbers and waves that Pax didn't understand. The name was clear: Miss Adams.

Yes! Pax clenched his fist. Then Roacher's film zoomed in on the face of the patient. There was a breathing tube inserted in her mouth and her eyelids were taped closed. Was Miss Adams still in a coma? Pax's joy at finding her evaporated in a flash.

Why were the teachers telling lies about Miss Adams making a good recovery and just needing rest? Pax didn't understand what was going on. And she couldn't do anything about the recent changes to the school if she never woke up.

Pax wanted to tell the others and wondered if they would be back for lunch soon. He looked at his watch but the screen was blank. With all that had been going on for the past few days he'd forgotten to charge up his wrist tab.

"Hey, Roacher, show me the time please."

The robot's eyes lit up again and beamed an image onto the wall once more.

PROPOFOL

"What's this, Roacher? I asked you the time."

The message on the wall disappeared but when Pax asked again what time it was, the same word appeared.

"That's weird," said Pax. "Have you picked up a glitch? Did Zach do something to you?" Checking on Roacher would have to wait. He rushed off to lunch, desperate to tell his friends what he'd learnt about the missing Head.

CHAPTER THIRTY-THREE

"She's in a coma?" Megan's mouth formed a perfect O as Pax relayed the news.

"That's terrible," said Briony, her face ashen. "Will she ever recover?"

Pax shrugged. "Don't know."

"OK, we've found her," said Samuel. "But what can we do about it now?"

"I don't know," Pax replied. But he knew it wasn't right. Like when he found something worth saving from a recycling lab, he just wanted to repair the headmistress. Make her whole again.

He didn't dare tell the others he was thinking like that. They'd probably think he was weird. He let it fester in the back of his mind, while his friends focused on the approach of the end of term. The late winter snow melted away, leaving behind the drooping petals of snowdrops as if the snow itself had created the flowers.

"Look, daffodils!" Megan squealed in delight at the appearance of the first yellow flowers of the year in the Victoria Gardens. A welcome splash of colour after the whites and greys of the past few months.

And best of all, the Parliamentary scoreboard showed the Judges were no longer in last place, which meant they wouldn't have extra duties for next term, and Pax might not get expelled after all.

While Pax continued to fret about Miss Adams, he also kept an eye out for Zachariah. Pax was still expecting some form of revenge for defeating him in the chess tournament but the school bully seemed oddly subdued.

"What you gonna do during the holidays?" asked Samuel as he packed his bags on the last day of term.

Pax shrugged. "I've got an idea for protecting Roacher. To make sure he doesn't get kidnapped again. But first I need to fix his software. He's been acting odd since I got him back from Zach. What about you?"

"Depends how me Dad is. London parade should be good. Might cheer him up with a bit of luck."

"See you in a couple of weeks then," said Pax.

[-]

The pupils staying at school over the holidays were allowed to use the labs for practice as long as they didn't make a mess. One of the third-year girls from Chancellors, Maria, was particularly keen on electronics, like Pax. Ordinarily, he would have liked to watch what she was doing, but he needed to work on Roacher alone, in secret. So, every morning he waited outside until she had finished her experiments before getting to work on his mechanical pet.

On the first day of the holidays, Pax upgraded the power of Roacher's battery. On the second day he added a voice-activated switch that connected the battery to the robot's outer shell. On the third day, he programmed in a special password to a new piece of software and lowered the output to its minimum setting. Pax picked up the robot and held it in his hand, nervous and excited both at the same time.

He spoke the password in a loud, clear voice. "Faraday."

Pax felt his hand tingle as an electric current hummed across Roacher's body. It was ticklish and he almost dropped the robot.

"Off."

He raised the output setting a notch and once again held out his hand.

"Faraday."

This time his hands juddered a little and catching sight of his reflection in a mirror, Pax saw that his hair was sticking up on end. "Off."

He raised the setting three more notches. He didn't dare test that level on himself.

I'd like to see Zach try to steal you now.

After lunch on that third day Pax took Roacher back to the computer lab. He wanted to investigate the glitch that was stopping the robot from telling the time any more.

Pax plugged Roacher into one of the main computers and ran some diagnostics on its solid-state drive. No malfunction detected. He checked the microprocessors but again they passed the health check. He knew it couldn't be the new software he'd just installed because the malfunction pre-dated that, so he called up the original programme he had used to code the robot and went through it line by line. It took him all afternoon. Still nothing. His stretched his aching back.

"What time is it?" he asked, rubbing his bloodshot eyes.

PROPOFOL

Pax groaned. Exactly the same word as before. How was that possible if there weren't any glitches in his software? Unless... maybe Roacher was trying to tell him something? Was propofol a proper word? What did it mean? The answer would have to wait for tomorrow. He was tired and hungry.

[-]

Pax found out the meaning of the mystery word in the library the next day. As its significance dawned on him, he ran to his room and used his wrist tab to call up his friends for a group call. Small images of Samuel, Megan and Briony appeared on his screen.

"Guys, listen up, I have some bad news. You remember that Roacher got that footage of Miss Adams in a coma? Ever since then, whenever I ask him the time, he just beams this word Propofol onto the wall."

"What's Pro-pa-full?" asked Megan.

"I've just found out. It's a drug they use in hospitals to knock out patients before they do operations. Anaesthetic is the fancy word."

168

"So?" said Samuel.

"It's also used to induce comas. Sometimes people get brought to hospital so badly injured the doctors want to keep them in a coma to help with rest and recovery. Especially if it's a head wound."

"Are you saying... Surely not?" said Briony

Samuel and Megan fell silent.

Pax nodded. "Somebody is keeping her in a coma on purpose. It has to be Old Leathery, so he can make changes to the school."

"Just to change our lessons? No way," said Samuel.

"It does seem a bit extreme," said Megan.

Pax rubbed the metal dots on the back of his head. "I know. But maybe they are only the start of what he wants to do with the school. It must be pretty major to go to all this trouble."

Pax's fingers and toes tingled all week as he tried to wrack his brains for something to try. He picked some flowers for Miss Adams and took them to the infirmary but the medical droid refused him entry. He looked around the entrance, wondering if he could sneak past the droid if he came back at night. But the droid wasn't the only thing guarding the entrance now.

A Beefeater was on sentry duty. The man was huge, taller than any of the robot teachers and nearly as broad as the doors into the ward, with a gun holstered on his belt. The guard stared at him so intently Pax felt like his very existence was an insult. He hurried back to the Judges' common room. The Beefeater's presence seemed to confirm the mayor's involvement. But what was he up to, and how was Pax going to rescue Miss Adams with a Beefeater in the way?

CHAPTER THIRTY-FOUR

The final week of the school holidays coincided with a week-long holiday for all New London's workers to thank them for their hard labour over the dark winter days. And it always started with a parade through the city of representatives from the Worshipful Companies as well as the Defence League and, on the river, the Thames Fleet.

Pax had seen the procession of floats a few times before. Even the workhouse kids got the day off to watch. Apparently, a show like this had been going on for more than five hundred years. Pax didn't see how they could have had floats in the old processions since the hover truck was only invented a few years ago. But the past was very confusing, and he didn't believe everything he read in history books.

The show was supposed to be a celebration of hard work but the ones Pax had seen always seemed to focus on the Lord Mayor himself. Which was ironic, since he probably did less work than anybody else in New London.

Pax wrapped up warm and spent Saturday lunchtime peering out of a window in St Stephen's tower on the West side of the school. He could see the crowds in Parliament Square waving at the passing open-top hover trucks. The Bakers were throwing cakes and doughnuts to the children. The Brewers were handing out cups of beer to the parents while other companies were demonstrating their skills with glassware, woodwork and other materials. Somebody was even having a haircut on the back of one of the hover trucks.

Usually, the procession circled around Parliament square before heading back East to the Guildhall. But this time Pax noticed that the Lord Mayor's coach broke off and pulled into the porch beneath Victoria Tower. When it left a few minutes later, the mayor was no longer on board.

Pax ran downstairs towards Central Hall, eager to see if he could find out why the mayor was visiting the school at this time, when nobody else was around. This was his chance to find out what the mayor was up to.

But there was no sign of the dignitary or his Beefeater guards by the time Pax reached the Long Gallery. Old Leathery couldn't have just disappeared. What was he up to? Where had he gone? Pax felt like he had no other choice. It was time for another midnight adventure.

[-]

He had already picked the lock on the door to the Judges' common room by the time Big Ben's deep voice announced it was midnight. Dressed all in black, wearing his night-vision goggles, Pax paused at each corner, waiting for Roacher to scuttle ahead and disable the security cameras. Eventually, Pax reached the night watchman's office near Central Hall and sent Roacher under the door.

Pax hid in the nearby storage cupboard, using near-field connectivity to watch the little robot's live feed. Pax had met the human guard who looked after the security droids before. Bill Everett. He didn't look like he'd ever be able to chase any intruders or put up much of a fight if the school was ever attacked. A reject from the Defence League, maybe? Whatever Bill's story, he wouldn't be adding to it this evening because he was fast asleep, snoring so loudly that Roacher's little antennae quivered from the vibrations.

The robot plugged itself into the monitoring system in the guard's office. Pax wiped sweaty palms on his trousers and took control from next door. He hunted out the video feed from earlier that day and found footage of the Lord Mayor entering the school at 14:14 and tracked his progress through the building.

At 14:16, The mayor entered Miss Adams' office and sat down at her desk. Pax could see the mayor's lips were moving, but the security cameras did not record sound. He tried to lip-read but couldn't work out what was being said, or to whom the mayor was talking. Nevertheless, Pax downloaded that section of video, hoping there would be some answers in this conversation, if he could figure out what was being said.

[-]

As the early morning sun washed the Eastern clouds pink, Pax went to the library to research lip-reading. The article he found said it was a skill that had been practiced for hundreds of years, but went on to explain how hard it was. The mouth and lips form only twelve different shapes while there are nearly 50 different sounds used in speech. So each shape is associated with several sounds and the art of lip-reading relies on figuring out which sound is most appropriate in the context of the rest of the speech.

Pax's eyes lit up when he read the second half of the article. In the past thirty years, advances in artificial intelligence had allowed computers to recognise all of the shapes easily (unless the speaker had a moustache or beard) and then quickly analyse the thousands of combinations of possible sounds to select the most likely sentence spoken. Pax found an American charity that had bought the rights to a lip-reading algorithm and was sharing it for free to help US citizens with hearing loss.

Yes! Pax banged his fist on the desk in delight.

After he had set up a fake American account, and rigged his internet access to make it seem as though he were connected in the US, Pax downloaded the software and used it to analyse the video of the mayor's conversation in Miss Adams' office.

He only got the mayor's half of the conversation but it didn't matter because the crucial information came straight from Silas Letherington's clean-shaven mouth.

Executive Order 163. Scholastic Parliament will be transformed into a Military Academy in September.

A pause. Then:

In order to prepare for this change, all pupils will have to pass training exercises based on the Defence League's officer development programme at the end of this forthcoming term.

Pax's fingernails bit into the palms of his hands as his knuckles whitened. He could scarcely believe it. After all that hard work in lessons during the year, the exams were going to be based on some stupid military exercises? Who would want that, except maybe for an idiot like Zachariah?

Even if Pax did pass the exam, what would be the point of staying at school? He didn't want to become a soldier, he wanted to become an engineer. That was the whole point of coming here in the first place. Pax felt sick at the prospect of his dreams being snatched away from him. This had to be stopped.

[-]

Pax thought about Executive Order 163 as he lay restless in bed that night. Roacher and Bee-Bop were chasing each other around the dormitory when the older robot slowed to a stop. Its music ceased and all but one of its lights faded.

"Good evening, Pax."

"Oh, it's you, Alderman. What do you want?"

"I would like you to stop sneaking around the school at night. There are only so many times I can ignore it."

"Somebody has been sneaking around again? Really?"

"You may have disabled the cameras, but I can follow the pattern in the outages."

"Aren't you the clever one." Pax used to think Alderman was on his side, but after all that happened last term and the zaps from his torc, he wasn't so sure. He was just glad he wasn't wearing his torc right now. "If you know it was me, why aren't you punishing me?"

"I am trying to help you become an Engineer."

"Hah, not if the mayor has anything to say about it."

"I want you to be an Engineer, Pax, so you can fix things. That is what you are good at."

"Then why are you going along with the mayor's interference in school?"

"I cannot refuse a direct order from him, but it does not mean I have to agree with everything he does."

Pax shook his head. "Pleased to hear it. But not much help, is it?"

"You know, in a huge ancient building like this, I would not be surprised if there were some forgotten passages that never had security cameras installed. Just a thought…"

"Huh?"

Bee-Bop's lights and music suddenly restarted, leaving Pax to ponder Alderman's meaning.

[-]

In the morning, Pax sent Samuel a direct message on Hansard, telling him about Executive Order 163.

> **SPF > Have your parents been consulted about any changes to the school?**
>
> **SamBan > No**
>
> **SPF >You're up on the rules. Can the mayor make whatever changes he wants?**

Pax rubbed the back of his head, as he waited for a reply.

> **SamBan > Dad says any change to the school's constitution has to be signed off by both the mayor & the head. If 1 of them is indisposed, say IN A COMA, an acting deputy can sign the Executive Order instead**
>
> **SPF > Acting head? That's Alderman!!!**

Since Pax knew that Alderman couldn't refuse a direct order from the mayor, its signature of approval was guaranteed at the end of term. After all the hard work last term avoiding last place in the Polls, now Pax wasn't sure it had been worth it. If Miss Adams didn't wake up in time, they were all going to end up in the army!

PART THREE

THE INFIRMARY

CHAPTER THIRTY-FIVE

T he friends gathered in the Judges' common room at the start of the new summer term. As Pax told Megan and Briony about Executive Order 163 and Samuel explained about Alderman being able to sign off on the executive order, the two girls held hands.

"I don't want to join the Defence League," said Briony. "I want to be a dancer."

"Why is the mayor doing this?" asked Megan.

Pax shrugged. "Anything in the news about him lately?"

"I found an article about the mayor's approval rating," said Samuel. "Some people are predicting he'll get voted out of office at next year's election"

"Shame the vote's not until next year," sighed Pax.

"I heard there's another Executive Order going through the Council this month," said Briony. "Order 162 is going to expand the Defence League and rename it as the Workers' Liberation Army."

"Sounds like the mayor is getting ready to take the war to the Countryside Alliance," said Megan.

"Maybe he thinks it will improve his ratings and get him re-elected," said Briony.

"He'll need lots more soldiers to win the war," said Samuel.

Pax clicked his fingers. "That's it! My friend Charlie, back in the workhouse, was caught up in a recruitment drive. And now it looks like the mayor's trying to get our school involved too. I overheard him talking with Miss Adams about how bad the outlook was. He refused to negotiate with the King but said he had another plan. I presumed he was going to use science to solve the problem. Now it seems like he's going to use force instead."

"What a whelk head!" shouted Megan, causing other Judges in the common room to look around at the four friends. "All this just so he doesn't lose his job?"

"We can't stop him if he wants a war," said Briony.

"Maybe not," said Pax. "But if we somehow rescued Miss Adams, we could at least stop him from turning our school into a military academy."

"How?" asked the others all together.

Pax thought about the Beefeater standing guard outside the infirmary and gulped. "I'm working on that."

[-]

The friends soon found out the end-of-term exams were going to involve a series of Capture-the-Flag games. There would be one match for each year of pupils. All four Parties would defend their own flag while attempting to capture as many of the other flags as possible. Points would be awarded and added to the Poll running totals.

The threat of expulsion still loomed over pupils in whichever Party came last. If the Judges did badly in these games, that would be Pax. He could barely sleep for the first week, terrified of either option: going back to the workhouse or staying on to train as a soldier.

How the Parties would fight each other became clear in the first PE lesson of the new term. Each pupil was given some moulded body armour covering their torso, with a large disc on the front and rear. There were helmets too, along with knee and elbow pads.

The PE instructor, Sir Geraint, wheeled around the gym checking everybody's protective clothing. "Now, the object of the exercise is to strike your opponent's disc or shoot it with a laser gun. You'll learn how to use the guns in the maths lesson this afternoon. This morning, we'll focus on using our fists and feet."

Pax groaned. He hated fighting. He knew Chen had taught Megan some self-defence skills before Christmas, but he'd not bothered asking to join in. And now she wasn't around to ask for help. Pax was beginning to regret that decision. And then felt guilty about missing Chen for purely selfish reasons, leaving a sour taste in his mouth.

"Pair up and start sparring," said Sir Geraint. "Remember, no aiming at the other person's face. Strike the disc to win the bout."

Pax wondered if he could try to just block the other person's punches all lesson. People started spreading out. Most of the girls wanted to spar against each other but Megan chose a boy who was one of Zachariah's friends.

"What's the matter, Ryan? Not scared of fighting a girl, are you?" She was up on the balls of her feet, arms flexed, fists clenched and held out with purpose. Pax looked across and saw the glint in her eye. Nope, he didn't fancy Ryan's chances. His smile quickly disappeared when he felt somebody tug on the straps of his body armour.

"Come on, Forby, let's dance." Zachariah squared up to him and pushed Pax back a couple of feet. Pax darted a look, left and right, wondering how to get out of this nightmare.

The bully struck a pose similar to Megan's stance then twisted sideways. He leant away from Pax and lashed out his right foot. As his leg straightened, the heel of his foot smacked straight into the disc in the middle of Pax's chest.

It happened so quickly, Pax hadn't even had a chance to try to block the attack. The blow didn't hurt too much thanks to the padding. But as he tumbled backwards, landing painfully on his bottom he felt a tingling all over his body, like a punishment from his torc. Only this was gentler, more numbing. He tried to get up but couldn't. He could still breathe and look around but none of his limbs would move.

Zachariah grinned. "Cool."

"Well done, Thomson. Now look class. See what's happened after Thomson struck Forby's disc. An electric impulse from his torc has immobilised Forby and a signal has been sent to Alderman. The effects will wear off after a few minutes but during the games, once you have been hit, you have to proceed to the Debating Chamber and wait for the end of your match."

Pax sat there, stiff as a statue, feeling stupid while the humiliation burned inside him.

"What if you just sneak off, Sir, and re-join the fight?" asked one of the Loyals who usually hung around with Zachariah.

"Alderman will know, and your Party will lose ten points. Plus, anybody you hit while cheating will be released and allowed to re-join their team mates. So, don't try it. OK, let's continue with the sparring. And don't forget there's a disc on everyone's back that does exactly the same thing as the front pad. If you can unbalance your opponent, it might be easier to strike there."

Sir Geraint de-activated Pax's torc and told him to try again. Pax wanted to run away but that would probably just get the Judges a penalty point, one they couldn't afford to lose. It didn't take long before Zachariah had struck once more. He was taller and stronger than Pax and clearly had trained in some form of martial art.

The repeated blows began to hurt, despite the padding and Pax could feel his anger and humiliation bubbling up, with nowhere to go. The only comfort was that out of the corner of his eye he could see Megan was having plenty of success against Ryan.

Sir Geraint showed the class some basic blocking techniques which everybody tried to copy, even though it was weird watching the robot's metal body and spindly arms twirl around. The teacher took pity on Pax and, for the next round, paired him up with Tshenolo, one of the girls from Peers. Both of them got the hang of blocking punches and kicks which just meant that neither of them could hit the other one's disc. By the end of the lesson, Pax was tired and sweaty inside the extra layer of padding. He was going to be useless in the end-of-term exams, he just knew it.

[-]

After a shower and lunch, the first years went to a gun-based maths lesson. Pax was even more appalled than in PE. This was worse than twitching hour! Once again, Zachariah showed his enthusiasm for the new curriculum by pushing to the front as the pupils filed into the classroom.

"What do guns have to do with maths?" asked Briony in an annoyed voice. She sounded even less keen on these new lessons than Pax.

"Isn't it obvious, Miss Latimer?" said Sir Tristram. "You need to work out your distances and angles, the movement of the target. It's all trigonometry."

The desks in the classroom had been pushed to one side and a row of discs, just like the ones attached to their body armour, had been hung on the far wall. Sir Tristram handed out five pistols to the first five pupils, which included Zachariah of course, and told them to stand behind the white line on this side of the room. When they were in position, the teacher started handing out safely glasses that would protect eyes against any stray shots.

"Looking after the pupils' pupils, eh Sir?" said Ravi Patel, the boy with the cheeky poem from the talent show.

"Yes, very good, Patel. Now," Sir Tristram turned to face those about to shoot, "set your feet shoulder width apart. Hold the gun in one hand and use the other hand to steady yourself. Look along the top of the barrel and squeeze the trigger gently. Remember this is just a laser, there's no bang or recoil to worry about."

The pupils assumed the stance and after the teacher suggested a couple of minor adjustments, they were declared ready.

"Let's see how many hits you can manage in a minute. The gun will only let you fire once every five seconds, so make every shot count."

Zachariah was annoyingly good. He got 11 out of 12 shots, far better than anybody else in the first group. Next up was Megan and Samuel. Megan struggled but Samuel's gaming skills obviously transferred over to this and he also got eleven hits.

Soon it was Pax's turn. The gun felt tainted in his hands. He couldn't imagine ever firing a gun for real. Neither he nor Briony were very good, scoring just six each. He picked at his lips, feeling useless. The first-year Judges had already lost their best fighter thanks to Chen's disappearance. And now Pax was convinced he would be a liability when it came to the final exams of the year.

[-]

As the days grew longer, Pax tried not to think of the forth-coming wargames, not wanting to take part and not wanting to face the consequences. He sat in the mullioned windows of the school and watched birds chasing insects or worms to feed their chicks. Red-breasted robins fought over territory, just like the mayor and the Pinchers. None of it made sense. He racked his brains, trying to think of a way to rescue Miss Adams.

The lessons in warfare dragged on. Geography lessons taught the pupils how to assess a location's vulnerability to attack, or what made certain places easier to defend. Pax didn't mind the abstract nature of a global chess board, but thinking about these tactics in a real environment turned his stomach.

In chemistry, Megan showed her aptitude in making smoke bombs. And of course, there was plenty of practice in close combat. Pax got a little better at defending himself and even managed to land the occasional feeble punch on Tshenolo's disc, knowing it wouldn't really hurt her. But everybody else in the class was improving too. And sometimes he couldn't avoid being paired up with Zachariah. The bully delighted in striking Pax where there was little or no body armour. Missing the disc meant Pax was not immobilised, but the bruises and the pain couldn't be switched off after the bout.

Gun lessons evolved. As everybody's accuracy improved, the teacher started introducing moving targets. Outside in one of the courtyards, Sir Tristram would throw a special globe into the air. Several pupils would have to track the ball simultaneously, as it spun and arced upwards, trying to hit it. It was easier to wait until the ball reached the top of its flight and started to slow but extra points were awarded for being the first in the group to register a hit. Fire too early and the chances were, you would miss. Fire too late and somebody else would probably gain the bonus. Pax's aim improved, but his hesitancy to fire kept cost-ing him points.

Over those first few weeks of the summer term, Pax tried time and again to find a way into the infirmary. Whenever he sent Roacher to spy on the medical ward, there was always a medical droid and a Beefeater on duty, even at night. While

Samuel slept, Pax lay awake in the dormitory, wracking his brains for a plan. They had to revive Miss Adams before the end of term.

In the darkness when sleep wouldn't come, Pax imagined going off to war with his grim-faced friends. How would he ever get to build and repair things as an engineer if he was in the Liberation Army? He just had to stop Executive Order 163.

CHAPTER THIRTY-SIX

Wwhile the others were all focused on practice for the upcoming capture-the-flag competition, Pax often retreated to his bedroom and distracted himself by playing with Roacher and Bee-Bop. Seeing the bigger robot recalled Pax's cryptic conversation with Alderman during the holidays. The super-computer had said something about secret passages and that he wanted Pax to fix things. Had he meant Pax's usual tech recycling skills or something bigger?

Maybe Alderman hoped Pax would rescue Miss Adams and was trying to help without breaking his programme protocols. Pax spent time in the library, searching for old maps of Westminster Palace. It had been burned down, rebuilt and extended, altered so many times over the ages, it was hard to find a definitive plan of the building. The more time Pax spent in the library, the more he began to enjoy the crinkle of old paper and its musty smell.

But with help from Miss Lucien, the librarian, Pax eventually found an account of the last architect to help with renovations to the building back in the twentieth century. He pretended to read the first few chapters and waited for Miss Lucien to return to her desk. Making sure nobody was watching, he unfolded a detailed map from the back of the leather-bound volume. He peered at the delicately inked lines.

Behind disguised doors, there were indeed several secret passages that criss-crossed the building. Some high up, others down in the cellars and basements. One even started at the cupboard known as the Caretaker's Coffin. Too complicated to memorise and too heavy to carry around, Pax used a camera to digitise the map and downloaded a copy onto the holo-frame cube Megan had given him for Christmas. So much had happened since then, that seemed a very long time ago.

He rushed back to his dorm, and began to study the digital copy of the map.

"Oi, stop reading, Pax!" said Samuel, entering the bedroom. "You shoulda been at laser-gun practice with the rest of us."

"I'm no good at that stuff," replied Pax.

Samuel crossed his arms. "All the more reason to practice."

"Look, I'm trying to find a way of getting to Miss Adams. During the capture-the-flag games, the medical droid will be looking after injured students in the debating chamber, instead of attending the infirmary. So that's my best chance of getting to our missing Head."

"Skipping the games, it's an automatic expulsion for you."

Pax frowned.

"And we're already missing Chen. Team is weak enough as it is," continued Samuel. "We're only nine points ahead of the Peers. Judges could easily end up back in last place if we do badly in the games."

"If I can't rescue Miss Adams, it doesn't matter who wins the Polls." But even as he said this, his stomach began to churn with worry. Samuel was right. If he didn't take part in the contest, he would be expelled. If the Judges came last, he would be expelled. And if he didn't rescue Miss Adams, he would end up in the army. Surely this was an impossible dilemma.

He asked Bee-Bop to play some soothing music while he tried to think of a solution. The corners of his mouth curled up as an idea began to form. Bee-Bop would need some bling, Roacher would need his sting and Pax would need Megan's help with a smoke bomb. But maybe, just maybe there was a way through this mess...

[-]

At breakfast time on the day of the final wargames, the temperature outside was already nudging 25 degrees and would soon top 30 according to the weather app on Pax's wrist tab. Not a great day to be donning thick body armour, helmets and pads.

The school cook had generously provided extra portions of toast, porridge and fruit, but most of the pupils had lost their appetite. Whether this was due to nerves or the metallic tang of London's factories wafting through the open windows was anybody's guess. Pax and his friends picked at their food, trying to nod and smile at each other but making very little conversation. The score in the Polls before these final games were displayed on the wall glass in the canteen.

LOYALS	240
CHANCELLORS	218
JUDGES	211
PEERS	202

The first round of competition would involve only pupils from the third year. While the rest of the school were asked to return to their common rooms, the four teams were given thirty minutes to select a place to plant their flag and set up any defences. Pax had thought about sneaking out to the infirmary now, but Alderman had stated that all pupils' movements would be monitored during the games through their torcs to ensure they stuck to the legitimate zone of conflict.

Pax was watching the action on the big screen in the Judges' common room along with his friends. He could see that three of the teams – including the Judges – had been very predictable and planted flags in their own courtyards. A few people around Pax tried to lead a round of cheering but the chanting was quickly replaced with a nervous silence.

The Loyals were being led by Hayley Robertson – the girl Pax had beaten in the semi-finals of the chess competition – and she chose a spot near the top of the south-east Tower. Pax could see their team setting up a barricade on the stairs. He gave a small nod of approval, even though it was the Loyals. "They're going for maximum defence this round, I just know it."

The rules of the game stated that if a team successfully defended its flag for the full two hours, they got 15 bonus points as well as ten points for each flag captured. The Loyals' captain had obviously decided to prioritise the defensive bonus. With their party holding a decent lead in the Polls, those fifteen points would likely be more than enough. Pax reckoned the Peers, currently in last place, would be desperate to get points off the Judges. He just hoped that wasn't going to happen.

A klaxon sounded throughout the school and the game began. It was hard to keep track of all the contestants' movements as the screen flicked between different cameras. It looked as though Pax was right – the Peers were going straight after the Judges' flag first. Their tactics were brutal and obvious. As pupils ducked in and out of doorways, laser guns fired down the corridors. Flashes of red seared across the screen, leaving vivid trails when Pax blinked.

His mouth tasted bitter as he watched the carnage. Stunned pupils turned into statues with faces frozen in anguish, clogging up the passageway. The two teams clashed in close combat. Fists and feet flung out in all directions. As the casualties mounted and neither side looked like winning, those still in the game backed away, leaving behind a tangle of living gargoyles.

But then the screen cut away to pictures of a small detachment of the Peers' team sneaking around the battle zone. They rushed the Judges' courtyard from the other side and quickly overwhelmed the last remaining defenders with a barrage of laser fire. The Peers' captain grabbed the flag and hoisted it aloft with a big grin. Back in the Judges' common room everybody groaned and Pax's knees sagged.

The cameras cut to the Chancellors' team. Most were staying near their own flag, hiding in defensive positions. A couple of them were sent off to scout for the Loyals' flag. One was zapped as she climbed the stairs in the south-east tower, while the other fled back to the rest of his team.

Before any of the teams could mount another attack, the klaxon sounded, setting off an alarm inside Pax's chest. The first round was over and the Judges were back in last place.

LOYALS	255
CHANCELLORS	233
PEERS	227
JUDGES	211

Over lunch Pax chatted to the captain of the Judges' second-year team, Philippa Green. All through the previous round, he'd been trying to come up with helpful ideas, using the strategies for combining defence with attack he'd learned when playing Global Chess. As round two began, the Judges' team ran off to set up their flag at the far end of Westminster Hall. Pax and his friends gathered in front of the screen in their common room. When the klaxon sounded most of the Judges' team sprinted towards the central lobby, leaving just two people in the huge hall.

"Two people can't defend the flag in there," said Samuel. "It's way too open."

"We've got to capture some flags this time, otherwise we'll never catch up," said Megan.

Pax patted Samuel's arm. "Don't worry, it's better protected than you think."

This time, the Peers concentrated their efforts on gaining the Chancellors' flag which had been placed in the corner of the canteen. The tables had been flipped over onto their sides and used as defensive barriers. Most of the Chancellors had stayed in place to defend.

It should have been a good base but as Pax watched the Peers creep closer to the canteen, he saw one of them throw a smoke bomb into the middle of the room. When it burst into thick grey clouds, the Peers charged forward.

"Sizzling circuits, that's smart," he said with a grim nod of his head.

It was hard to tell what was happening on the screen. The smoke pulsed red as laser guns were shot across the room. There were shouts and thuds as pupils from the two teams wrestled each other to the floor. When the smoke cleared, there were a dozen new statues but two people from Peers were smiling for the camera, holding the Chancellors' flag.

The view on screen cut to the Peers' flag, positioned in their courtyard again. A boy and a girl were crouching down next to the door that led to the party. The Judges' team were sneaking along the corridor, getting ready to launch an attack. Pax gestured to the screen. He wanted to shout out where the defenders were hiding. He just hoped Phillipa had a plan.

"Come on, Phillipa," shouted Briony, shattering the nervous silence in the Judges' common room.

The cameras cut back to Westminster Hall.

"Don't change cameras," said Megan. "We needed to see—"

She gasped as it became clear what was happening. Four of the Loyals' team were sneaking into the hall, getting ready to capture the Judges' flag.

Samuel turned to Pax. "You better be right 'bout our flag."

Pax nervously rubbed the metal dots on the back of his head as the Loyals began to sprint the length of the hall. Two laser guns lashed out with red tongues at the back of the attackers and a pair of Loyals became frozen to the spot. The other two didn't stop to fire back but kept running towards the Judges' flag. Just like in the maths lessons, it would be another five seconds before the guns could shoot again.

Briony grabbed Pax's hand. "They'll never stop them now."

Pax forgot all about the games, Miss Adams, even the threat of expulsion. Briony was holding his hand. And just for a moment, that was all that mattered.

The two remaining Loyals got within ten metres of the end of the hall. The raised platform where the Judges' flag stood proud was almost within touching distance. The pair of Judges giving chase were not closing fast enough. Just as the Loyals were about to mount the platform, they both fell flat on their faces. The camera zoomed in to show a trip-wire stretched across the hall just in front of the stage. The Judges swooped down like preying eagles and smacked the discs on the back of the fallen Loyals. A huge cheer erupted from the common room.

"Cor! Never doubted you for a minute, mate," said Samuel going for a high-five. Pax hastily let go of Briony's hand as his cheeks flushed red.

The camera switched to the south-east tower. The captain of the Chancellors was hoisting the captured flag of the Loyals above her head, surrounded by smoke, statues and some grinning fellow Chancellors. The claxon sounded for the end of that round. The Judges' attack against the Peers had run out of time.

"At least we our defended flag and scored some points," said Briony.

"But we're still in last place," pointed out Samuel. They all looked towards the score board, trying to figure out if they could yet catch the others.

LOYALS	255
PEERS	252
CHANCELLORS	243
JUDGES	226

"There are plenty of points on offer," said Megan with a smile that didn't quite reach her eyes.

"And Miss Adams is still in a coma," replied Samuel, looking at the ground.

Pax was running out of time.

CHAPTER THIRTY-SEVEN

The first years had been allowed an early tea. Everybody in the Judges' team picked at their macaroni cheese, but Pax tried to encourage them. "We'll need the energy."

"Try telling me stomach that," said Samuel.

Megan looked up and down the table at the other ten people in their team. "Pax, we've all agreed that you should be our Captain."

Pax blinked, a forkful of pasta halfway to his mouth.

"Mate, you smashed it in the chess competition," said Samuel. "We need some of that magic right now if we're gonna catch the other parties."

Pax struggled to swallow his food. His throat felt tight. A leader. He never thought he'd be capable of this. Finally, he smiled. "OK, if you're sure. I do have a couple of ideas. But if we're going to get everything we can out of this round, it'll be risky."

Everyone murmured their agreement.

"We'll discuss more back in the common room. Come on, eat up."

[-]

Pax outlined his plan for the final game to the rest of the team as everyone put on their body armour and helmets. The heat of the day had seeped into the core of the building and there was nowhere to escape it. Putting more layers on felt as unbearable as asking for extra homework.

"We're going to place our flag at the top of Victoria Tower, tied to the real school flag, but leaving nobody up there to protect it."

"That's crazy," said Harriet, Chen's roommate.

"Hiding in plain sight is more effective than you think," said Pax. "And besides, if we're going to get all the flags, we need everyone on attack. In global chess, if you throw everything at your opponent, they're too busy defending to attack you back."

Pax continued to explain how they would go about capturing the other teams' flags. After the team had dispersed to get ready, Pax told Samuel, Megan and Briony about his own mission – sneaking off mid-game to try to resuscitate Miss Adams.

"Why couldn't you have done it during the earlier games?" Megan asked.

"Because all the main corridors are being monitored and I'd have been spotted before I got anywhere near the infirmary."

"So how are you going to get there during our game?" asked Samuel.

"You don't want to know. But what's important is that you all concentrate on getting the other three flags. That's the only way we stand a chance of catching up the other Parties and not finishing last."

[-]

When Alderman announced that the first-year game was about to begin, Pax and the rest of the team huddled together. Despite carrying the weight of the whole school on his shoulders, Pax found he wasn't being crushed. There was an inner steel that hadn't been present six months ago. Samuel was handed the flag and when the timer started for the thirty minutes of preparation time, he ran for the tower.

"Now remember, Megan," said Pax, "if anything happens to me, you're in charge. Stick to the plan, OK? You can do this."

"We can do this," she said, "together."

Pax a felt twinge of sadness and then nodded. Everybody checked their guns. When Samuel came back, he was grinning.

"One of the Loyals tried to follow me, but I led 'em away from the tower and once I'd lost 'em, doubled back."

"Well done," said Briony.

"OK Samuel, when the klaxon sounds, use your drone to help find the Peers' and Chancellors' flags. I'll go scout out the Loyals."

"I'm not cheating," said Samuel.

Pax shook his head. "It doesn't say anything in the rules about looking for the flags with a drone. We just can't steal one with it."

Samuel looked impressed. "Nice one."

The klaxon sounded and the game began.

The Judges' team split into three. Megan and five others started to scout out the eastern corridors that overlooked the Thames. Briony and three more stayed with Samuel while he flew a drone around the outside of the school looking for spots where the other teams' flags might be. Pax, meanwhile, sneaked off on his own.

He ran off, heading for Zachariah's most likely base: the Long Gallery. As he got closer, Pax's feet slowed but his heart beat quickened. He crept between doorways, keeping an eye on the corridor ahead. Every time he heard a noise, he threw a nervous look behind him. He stuck to the shadows whenever he could, but the summer sun stabbed through the windows like a blade of heat. Perspiration dripped down the inside of Pax's helmet as he stood outside the Long Gallery and his gun handle felt slippery in his sweaty palm.

This was the site of his victory in the chess competition and he knew there was a podium at the far end of the room that might have been fortified by Zachariah. Pax ducked his head around the door frame and peeked inside. Yes! There it was. The Loyals' flag.

He risked another, longer look. No guards? Maybe Zachariah was going on the attack, hoping to capture other flags quickly before the Judges could get them. The Loyals' flag, a white shield with a red cross, hung limply in the still, warm air of the Gallery. It was so tempting, just standing there, behind a couple of up-turned tables and some chairs. He patted a pocket. "Roacher, stay out of sight, OK?"

Pax took a deep breath and sprinted towards the podium. Two Loyals jumped up from behind the barricade. They raised their guns. Pax dived to one side and let off a quick shot that was hopelessly off target. He tried to calm his breathing and counted to five as he scrambled for cover behind a row of chairs.

Before he got to four, a pair of strong hands had grabbed him from behind, pinning his arms to his side. He gasped as the gun was knocked from his grip and Pax was pulled into the middle of the room. The boy and the girl behind the barricade covered him with their guns, a smug grin on both their faces. The person holding him spun Pax around until he faced his nemesis: Zachariah.

"Honestly, Forby. That's got to be the oldest trick in the book. Pretending to leave your flag undefended." The boy shook his head in a rueful laugh. "And we all thought you were the tactical genius."

"You haven't won yet," said Pax, jutting his chin forwards and up.

"Nope, but I do get to have a little fun." Zachariah smirked. When Pax didn't move, he beckoned him forward. "Come on, pinhead. Just you and me. The rest of them promise not to fire. So, if you beat me, they'll let you go, OK?"

Pax felt his arms being released. He'd never beaten Zachariah in any of their sparring bouts. The bully was just toying with him. But this was also part of Pax's plan. Bracing himself for the inevitable pain, Pax took a step forward. Wham!

Zachariah had lunged forward and jabbed his fist straight into Pax's face. His nose felt like it was on fire and his eyes began to water. He couldn't see a thing. He tried to hold his hands in front of his disc to protect himself.

"Oops, did I miss your disc?" said Zachariah.

Pax felt something warm drip down onto his top lip. He licked it and tasted iron. A memory flashed into his mind – dangling from the top of Mandela Farm many months ago, just as helpless as he was now. As Pax tried to blink away his tears, Zachariah jabbed again. Pax blocked, but when his arm pushed the first punch away, the other boy used his long reach to swing a follow-up punch with his left hand. It connected with Pax's disc and his limbs went rigid.

Pax stood there, frozen to the spot. Blood was dripping from his nose, down and around his lips where it pooled before dropping to the floor. Pax knew it had to be this way, but that didn't lessen the fear of helplessness gripping his insides. Whoops and laughter echoed around the room. Zachariah filled Pax's field of vision with the bully's face only inches from his own.

"Better luck next time, Forby. I'm going to enjoy getting the rest of your team and capturing your flag." Zachariah took Pax's helmet off and patted him on the head. "Be a good boy and toddle off to the debating chamber when it wears off. Oh, and in case you were thinking of cheating, I'm leaving Susan here to escort you back."

Pax stood there, humiliated and hurt. He was out of the game.

CHAPTER THIRTY-EIGHT

P ax's nose was throbbing and as the blood congealed, it began to itch. He was desperate to scratch his nose, but the only thing he could move were his eyes and his lungs. In training, the teachers had said the paralysis would wear off after five minutes but right now it felt like five hours. Pax wondered how his team mates were getting on.

Megan should be in charge now. She knows the plan. It's a good plan. It will still work. It might work.

Caught in the middle of the Long Gallery, frozen to the spot with an itchy nose as distraction, Pax was finding it hard to maintain his optimism.

His legs and arms began to tingle. It was like the feeling he sometimes got when he slept on an arm and on waking, the circulation surged back. Relief and pain at the same time. His limbs were warming up quickly and Pax realised that he could wiggle his toes. He willed his hand towards his nose and it actually moved. When he rubbed it, he could feel blood starting to drip again. He stopped scratching.

"Time for you to leave," said the Loyal first-year girl who had stayed behind to guard him. "You know the rules, straight back to the debating chamber." She chuckled to herself. "Along with all the other losers."

Pax obeyed, turning away as he tried to suppress a grin. He could hear her steps behind him, following all the way to the neutral zone where pupils who were out of the game had to wait. This was exactly where he needed to be for the second part of his plan. It had made winning the capture-the-flag game harder, but from here he might just be able to rescue Miss Adams and therefore save the whole school.

When he entered the debating chamber – the bench-filled grand room that was used for school assemblies – he saw Miss Bowie and a few pupils from Peers and Chancellors. No other Judges here yet. That was good. But no Loyals either. Not so good.

The medical droid wheeled itself towards Pax, the same robot who had stopped Pax from entering the infirmary all term. "Sit down please while I tend to your injury."

Pax did as he was told. He closed his eyes as the droid cleaned his nose and checked it over. "I suspect you'll have a couple of black eyes in the morning. Nothing broken, though."

Now for a crucial part of the plan. "Can I take my torc off please?" he asked, trying to suppress the quake in his voice. "My neck feels a bit bruised."

"Affirmative." There was a click from the lock on Pax's torc.

Pax removed the metal band, rubbed at his neck and smiled. Now, as long as he stayed away from the cameras, the school had no way of tracking him. He looked up at the big screen that was showing progress in the first years' game. There was a scoreboard next to the screen which showed the running total with points added for the current game, as it stood at the moment. Pax clenched his fist as he realised that Megan and the rest of the team must have captured the Peers' flag. The Judges were still in last place but were only one point behind the Peers.

LOYALS	270
CHANCELLORS	258
PEERS	252
JUDGES	251

The medical droid went over to tend to a girl from Peers who had just limped into the debating chamber. Pax wandered towards the raised throne that Miss Adams used to occupy during assemblies. He kept an eye on Miss Bowie and the pupils in the chamber. Everybody's attention was on the screen, watching the contest unfold. The medical droid was strapping up the leg of the girl who had just entered.

Pax knew there was a secret passage hidden somewhere behind the throne from studying the palace map he had found. It would take him down to a corridor in the basement and then up a narrow spiral staircase to the reception desk of the infirmary. He ducked behind the huge throne and looked for the concealed panel.

His heart squeezed tight when he couldn't see anything obvious. It had to be there! His whole plan depended on it. Running his fingers over the intricate carvings, he tried to stay out of sight from the rest of the room. A faint breeze blew across his face. He put a finger in his mouth and used its wetness to help detect where the draught was coming from. Yes! There! A slight gap in the panels.

A carving next to the gap stuck out a little more than the others, worn from hands that had rubbed it countless times through the ages. Pax reached out to twist it and heard a quiet click. The panel hinged back and then stuck, half-open. He'd found the door, thank goodness! Pax squeezed through the narrow gap and shut the door behind him as quickly as possible. It was pitch black.

"Roacher, I need your lights."

The little robot crawled out from under Pax's body armour and settled on his shoulder. Pax switched on Megan's holo-frame and began to follow the secret route. With help from Roacher's blue beams, he made his way carefully along the dim passage, down age-worn steps. The musty smell of damp wafted past him on a faint breeze. The air was cooler down here in the basement. He shivered inside his sweaty padded clothing. Pax hurried forwards in a stooping jog, trying to avoid getting his head tangled up in cobwebs as he followed the ancient walkway.

Eventually, Pax crept from the secret door behind the infirmary's reception desk, which was unmanned, as expected. But the Beefeater was still guarding the doors into the treatment rooms. Pax could hear some yells from down the corridor and thought he recognised Megan shouting instructions. The noise faded as the battle moved away. Pax turned to peek at the

Beefeater from behind the desk, hoping he'd been distracted. The man hadn't moved a muscle.

Pax reached inside his pocket and pulled out the spherical smoke bomb Megan had made for him. He pressed a small red button on top of the bomb and, staying out of sight, rolled the ball towards the guard. The bomb popped open and dark grey clouds expanded rapidly to fill the area in front of the infirmary's double doors.

"Oi, no fighting in here," cried the Beefeater. "This is out of bounds."

There were certain parts of the school that were off limits to Capture-the-Flag contests and this was one of them. Pax placed Roacher on the floor and watched the little robot disappear into the thick smoke which was starting to thin already.

"Hurry!" he whispered.

A pair of large red eyes glowed within the clouds. Uh-oh! The Beefeater must be wearing a special mask. The eyes looked down and Pax saw a hand lurch towards the floor.

"Gotcha! Not sneaking past me, little droid."

Pax could see Roacher's antennae sticking out of one of the Beefeater's massive hands. He could almost feel the guard's hand around his own heart, squeezing tight just like he was gripping Roacher. All the dread he'd felt when Zachariah had captured Roacher came flooding back, dousing Pax with cold water.

The guard looked up as he saw the boy approaching. "Might have known it would be you. Didn't think I'd spot your little pet, did you?"

Pax kept walking closer.

"You're in for it now. The Lord Mayor's gonna—"

"Faraday," said Pax, loud and clear.

The guard's face creased in confusion as a flash of blue light briefly illuminated the room. Pax had made sure the setting on Roacher's body was ramped up to its maximum. The guard's body juddered for a few seconds and then slumped to the floor. As the clouds dissipated, Pax could see the Beefeater flat out on his back and Roacher standing tall on the man's chest, with his antennae out straight. The Beefeater's face was covered with some sort of respirator and red goggles which had protected him from the smoke but not from Roacher's new electric zapper.

Pax scooped up the robot and stepped through the doors into the medical ward. He found Miss Adams' room and entered on tip toe, as if he didn't want to disturb her sleep. But it was hard to keep quiet. He wanted to jump about and scream with joy. He'd got here at last!

There was a tube sticking out of her nose and some wires attached to her head and one of her fingers. A bag of clear liquid hung off something that looked like a skinny hat stand. Pax could see another tube leading from the bag into the back of Miss Adams' left hand. It had to be the Propofol. He closed off the tap, removed the tape from her eyelids and brushed a stray hair away from her face. He sat down to wait, hoping his Headmistress would wake before the Beefeater did.

The minutes ticked by, even more slowly than when he had been immobilized in the Long Gallery. Pax stared at Miss Adams, hoping to see some sign of life. After a few minutes of nothing, he shifted in his chair, noticing a wall glass facing Miss Adams's bed. Pax turned it on. Images of the ongoing competition filled the screen. The Polls in the bottom right-hand corner showed that the Judges' score had gone up another ten points and the Chancellors had lost their defensive bonus. Pax jumped out of his seat and punched the air. Yes! Megan and the team had done it again. Now they just needed to defend their own flag, and they wouldn't finish last in the Polls. Pax hoped Megan would remember to switch tactics.

LOYALS	**270**
JUDGES	**261**
PEERS	**252**
CHANCELLORS	**243**

There was a groan from Miss Adams and her eyelids flickered. Pax turned away from the screen, as hope lifted his heart once more. He watched her for a few moments but there was nothing else. He bit his lip and turned back to the screen.

Come on, guys, you can do it!

"Pax?"

He turned again to see Miss Adams trying to sit up. At last! A flood of relief washed over him like a ray of sunshine. He helped prop her up with a pillow, trying to control his emotions. None of them were safe yet.

"What am I doing in the infirmary? And why are you in my room, wearing that armour? What are those pupils on the screen running around for?"

Pax smiled at the Headmistress. "I have a lot to explain."

Before he managed to start his explanation, a beep came from the monitor, announcing a change in the score. The Judges' score had just dropped by fifteen points and the Chancellors' score had gone up by ten.

LOYALS	270
CHANCELLORS	253
PEERS	252
JUDGES	246

An image from the top of Victoria Tower showed the smallest boy in the whole senior school grinning next to the Judges' grey boulder pennant. The decision to leave the Judges' flag unattended was looking like a massive mistake. If the Judges failed to get the Loyals flag in the next ten minutes, they would remain last in the Polls. Which meant Pax might have saved the school but not himself. He was still heading for expulsion.

CHAPTER THIRTY-NINE

Pax held his head in his hands. To have come so close but to miss out now... He tried to take comfort from knowing the headmistress would be back in charge of the school. But with seedlings in the losing party always chosen to be expelled, he wouldn't be around to share that joy. Back to Workhouse Five and whatever punishments Hairy Hanson had lined up for him.

"What's wrong Pax?" asked Miss Adams.

Pax explained about the Capture-the-Flag competition, with the laser guns and the armour. She was appalled.

"But what about your end-of-year exams?"

"They don't fit into the Lord Mayor's plans for the school. But if we can get you past that Beefeater, you can stop the Executive Order."

"Beefeater? Here in the school? What Executive Order?"

Pax did some more rapid explaining. He tried to keep an eye on the screen and talked quickly, but Miss Adams was still rather dazed and struggling to keep up with events.

"You mean I've been lying here since Christmas? All because of Silas, that jumped up, horrid little squirt?"

Pax smirked. He didn't think he'd ever heard an adult be so rude about the Lord Mayor before. Miss Adams tried to sit up, but her muscles were weak and stiff after too long in bed. She collapsed back down onto her pillow.

"Take it easy, Miss." Pax was trying to keep calm but his glances out into the corridor were becoming more frequent. The Beefeater was going to be awfully angry when he awoke. And Pax knew his friends were almost out of time to capture the Loyals' flag. He turned to watch the screen again. The image of the Long Gallery showed at least seven of Zachariah's team crouched behind benches and tables, ready to defend their flag from the inevitable final attack. The Loyals would win the Polls once again if they maintained their defensive bonus. And the Judges would finish last. The clock showed three minutes left.

The camera zoomed in on a droid wheeling its way into the Long Gallery. It was small and shaped like a bin on wheels with a domed, silver top. The Loyals held back for a moment, unsure what this thing was. But Pax knew. It was the extra help he'd recruited to make up for him being out of the game: Bee-Bop, with a shiny new head. When Pax's robot companion was in the middle of the gallery, lights started flashing on its body and music started playing from its hidden speakers. The effect was a bit like laser gun fire, even though it was all perfectly harmless.

"Oi! That's not allowed!" shouted one of the Loyal defenders.

A boy with short black hair, stood up and fired his laser gun at Bee-Bop. The silver dome acted as a mirror. The shot bounced back towards the boy who dived for cover. Seeing their friend get attacked other Loyals stood up and fired at Bee-Bop. But that just resulted in more shots bouncing off his dome and a couple of the defenders had their discs hit and were frozen to the spot.

"Stop shooting! Stay down!" shouted Zachariah. But the others were panicked by now and continued firing a little longer. "I said can it, you whelk-heads!" That was when Samuel, Briony and four other Judges charged into the room and a huge gun battle began.

Watching through the screen it was hard for Pax to tell who was winning. He could have sworn somebody had zapped Zachariah's disc but the bully kept on firing and shouting. Somehow, he had not been immobilised. Bee-Bop tried to make a nuisance of itself, whizzing around the room, banging against the legs of the Loyal defenders. One of them looked down at the robot, giving Samuel enough time to punch their disc.

"Good old Bee-Bop!" shouted Pax, causing Miss Adams to jump in surprise.

Briony shot two of the Loyals, but another one shot her. The room was becoming crowded with living statues.

Bee-Bop tried to distract Zachariah but the boy flicked the robot onto its side and stamped down hard on its metal body. The cylinder crumpled inwards and sparks flew out as Bee-Bop's music faded and its wheel stopped spinning.

Pax leapt up from his chair and reached out a hand to the screen. "No!" He could barely breath, as if Zachariah had booted him in the stomach. The pain was doubled by the knowledge that he had sent his own robot into battle, even with the risk that something like this might happen. But there had been no other way.

The camera remained focused on the bully who was grinning as Samuel came charging towards him. Pax had never seen his friend so angry. His nostrils flared and his white eyes seemed enormous under the rim of his helmet.

"Oh, sorry. Did I break it?" said Zachariah.

Samuel raised his gun and fired it straight at the bully's disc. Pax could see it was a direct hit, but again nothing happened. That was when he realised the circle was a slightly different colour to everyone else's disc. What was going on?

Zachariah pouted his lip. "Oh dear, didn't it work?"

"You cheatin' BLEEEEPP." The school video edited out Samuel's swearword.

"Tut, tut, Samuel. Language like that will lose you points." Zachariah settled into a stance with his legs apart, knees flexed and hands raised in front of him. He beckoned for Samuel to approach. As his friend did so Pax could see a Loyal girl sneaking up behind Samuel. She raised her gun. Pax yelled at the monitor even though he knew it couldn't help.

The camera cut back to a view of the entrance to the Long Gallery as Megan ran into the room and shouted a warning to Samuel. The Loyal girl turned to face Megan and shot her gun. But Megan was too fast. She ducked and rolled behind one of the up-turned tables as the laser gun zapped harmlessly into the desk. She stood up and fired. The Loyal girl went rigid.

"Yes!" Pax jumped up and punched the air.

Just for a moment, Samuel had let himself be distracted by the girls' fight. He didn't even notice Zachariah edge closer towards him. Megan tried to yell another warning but it was too late. The Loyals' leader lashed out his foot and kicked the disc on the back of Samuel's body armour. The room fell silent as Pax's roommate froze. It was just Megan versus Zachariah and only one minute to go.

"It's quite exciting, isn't it?" said Miss Adams.

Pax turned to look at the Headmistress and bit his lips, fighting the urge to scream.

Megan advanced slowly on Zachariah. He resumed his fighting stance. She ran forward and tried to somersault past the boy, towards the flag. Zachariah watched her soar through the air and swung his leg out, timing it perfectly to catch her in the stomach as she landed. It missed her disc but Megan staggered backwards, winded.

Zachariah's eyes danced with grim pleasure and he reached out a hand to grab her ponytail. His hand swished at thin air as Megan ducked down and she swept Zachariah's feet from under him. He tumbled to the floor, face down. Megan reached over and while he struggled to get back up, she struck the disc on his back. Zachariah stopped wriggling.

"Yes!" Pax shouted at the screen. He turned to throw his arms around Miss Adams and then realised what he was about to do and sat back down, looking at the clock on the screen. Ten seconds to go!

Megan ran up to the raised platform where the Loyal flag had been planted, but fell flat on her face. Pax could see a trip wire running across the room, between two posts. The Loyals had used Pax's trick on his own team. "Get up," he shouted at the screen. "Get up!" He stood and walked towards the screen as if that might help.

Megan groaned and tried to rise. One of her legs buckled and she fell back down. Pax groaned as the clock showed five seconds to go. Megan started to crawl across the platform and dragged herself up. The flag was nearly in reach of her outstretched arm. One last heave and the klaxon sounded at exactly the same time as the monitor bleeped to announce a change of score. Megan's fingertip was on the flag. They had gained an extra ten points and the Loyals had lost their defensive bonus.

Pax could not believe it. There was a bubble of something in his throat that wasn't food or air. The screen went blurry as he tried to take in what had just happened. When he blinked them away, the scoreboard showed that the Judges weren't in last place anymore. Not just that, they had actually won the Polls by a single point. Despite the tears, he couldn't ever remember feeling quite so happy.

JUDGES	256
LOYALS	255
CHANCELLORS	253
PEERS	252

The door to Miss Adam's room banged open.

"YOU are not supposed to be in here. And YOU are not supposed to be awake." The Beefeater's voice boomed from the doorway.

Pax snapped out of his moment of joy, feeling hot and angry. The mayor was not going to take away their victory now, right at the last. He stood up, blocking the way to Miss Adam and swung a punch at the Beefeater. He wasn't tall enough to aim for the man's face, so Pax drove his fist towards the man's stomach instead. It bounced painfully off a wall of pure muscle. The Beefeater reached out an arm and swept Pax into the side wall. "I'll deal with you later," the man said as he advanced on the headmistress.

"How dare you," she said, trying to sit up. The Beefeater pushed her back down with one hand and turned the tap on her drip with the other. She squirmed under his hand but he was too heavy and too strong.

Pax watched in a daze. He had smacked his head against the window frame when the Beefeater had pushed him aside. There was a ringing in Pax's ears and he was finding it incredibly hard to come up with a new plan.

Miss Adams stopped struggling and Pax thought it was a bit of a shame to have got quite so close. He had nearly saved the school. But now was a good time for a rest. Just a quick nap, here against the cold, hard wall. It was surprisingly comfortable. As his vision faded and he slipped towards the floor, Pax dreamt of a knight in shining armour riding to the rescue.

CHAPTER FORTY

P ax was lying in bed with his eyes closed, half-awake but not trying very hard to emerge fully from his slumber. A faint smile tugged at his lips as memories of a wonderful fairy-tale dream danced across the inside of his eyelids. Something about giants and knights. His face felt warm as sunlight caressed his cheek. The sun never reached the bed in his dorm. Where was he? His eyes snapped open.

"Good morning, young Forby."

A medical droid appeared in his field of vision, but it hadn't been an electronic voice that had spoken to him.

"You can leave us now," said the voice again and Pax recognised it as Miss Adams. She wasn't in a coma anymore! He sat up quickly and winced as his head throbbed with the effort. "Take it slowly, Pax. That was quite a knock you received."

Pax blinked and looked around the room. Their roles had been reversed. The Headmistress was dressed and he was in his pyjamas lying in a bed in the infirmary. "How long have I been asleep?"

"About 18 hours."

"The Beefeater? What happened to him?"

"Although you couldn't stop him, your valiant stand gave me just enough time to send an alert to the staff. Sir Lancelot came to my rescue."

Pax shook his head. "I thought I'd dreamt that bit."

"No point in having a school full of knights if they can't fight, hey?"

"What about the executive order? To change the school."

Miss Adams put a hand on the bedsheet next to Pax's arm. "Fear not. Alderman had been holding back from signing it for as long as possible. And once I was awake, the mayor knew I would never sign it, so he dropped the whole idea."

"Why didn't he just sack you, instead of all going to all this trouble?"

She smiled. "Ah, well, that's up to the school's board of governors, not the mayor. One of the few things he doesn't control in New London. He is furious of course, but keeping a low profile for now. If the parents knew he'd drugged me and tried to convert the school without consultation, they'd be on the war path."

"Why don't we tell them? Get him kicked out of office? I remember what you called him…"

For the first time ever, Pax saw the Headmistress' cheeks flush red. "I'm hoping I can count on you not to repeat that to anybody, please. Unfortunately, we can't get rid of Silas Letherington that easily. We don't have any real proof of what he has been up to."

"Really?" said Pax.

"Yes. Somehow, the system has already deleted any reference to Executive Order 163. And Propofol *is* sometimes used to help patients with head injuries." She touched the back of her head where she'd fallen all those months ago.

Pax clenched his jaw, but that made the inside of his head pound again. It was infuriating to think the Lord Mayor was going to escape punishment.

"The main thing is, young man, that thanks to you and your friends, there's still a school to come back to next year. They're outside now, if you're up to receiving some visitors?" said Miss Adams.

Pax smiled and nodded as he tried to sit up again. Samuel burst into the room a moment later followed by Briony, both of them grinning like idiots.

"You did it, guys!" He tried to find the words to express how grateful he was but he just couldn't. "That was some battle in the Long Gallery," he said eventually.

Samuel bumped fists with his friend. "All your plan, mate. Sacrificing yourself at the start so you could rescue Miss Adams. That was urbane." Samuel stood back to look at his friend. "You know you look like a panda? How's yer conk?"

Pax put a hand to his face. His nose was sore to touch. He realised there wasn't a mirror in the room. The medical droid had talked about a pair of black eyes yesterday. "S'OK," he shrugged.

Briony bashed Samuel on the shoulder. "He doesn't look like a panda." She leant forward and kissed him on the cheek. "We're very proud of you."

Pax felt all his pain melt away like ice cream in sunshine.

"Aww, now come on. I've only just had me lunch," said Samuel, sticking a finger down his throat and pretending to gag.

"Hang on," said Pax. "Where's Megan?"

"A bit slower than last time you saw her," Briony replied.

The doors thudded open and Megan hobbled forwards, two crutches tip-tapping across the floor. Her left ankle was covered in a big white cast.

"That looks sore," said Pax.

"You looked in a mirror recently?" she replied.

Pax grinned. "That fight with Zachariah was awesome."

"Yeah well, wasn't going to let that drewgi beat us, was I?"

"I still have no idea what a drewgi is," said Pax, shaking his head. He looked around the room at his three friends. He couldn't remember ever being quite so happy.

[-]

Pax was allowed out of the infirmary in time for the final assembly of the school year. Miss Adams was back in her rightful place, on the throne in the debating chamber. The red leather benches were packed with students. The Parliamentary scoreboard was displayed on the wall above Miss Adams' head and the Judges were cheering like mad, while the Peers all sat in silence.

After spending so long worrying it would be him getting expelled at the end of term, Pax found it hard to celebrate too much, knowing the future of the students in Peers rested on a simple twist of fate. It was such a cruel system.

"Order! Order!" Miss Adams stood up as the grand hall fell into silence. "Now, it is too late to change what happened this term, but know this. Next year we will be reverting to our traditional core subjects and our normal examination system."

Some of the students, including Pax, cheered at this announcement.

She continued. "There will be plenty of summer homework to catch up on all the lessons you missed during my absence."

A huge groan filled the room.

"But first, we have the Parliamentary Polls to award."

The Judges pounded their feet on the floor and cheered. Pax could feel the noise through his feet and chest. He grinned as Samuel slapped him on the back.

Miss Adams stared over at them all until the noise stopped. "I have some minor adjustments to make to the scores."

Murmurs filled the room as Pax shifted uncomfortably in his seat and the Peers leant forward in their seats, grim faces looking hopeful.

"Video footage of the final game has been reviewed after we received a complaint from the Loyals," continued the Head. "The Judges use of a simple droid for distraction purposes has been ruled entirely legal."

The Judges all cheered and Pax clenched a fist, even as the thought was tinged with sadness for his broken robot.

"But," said Miss Adams, "the Judges *are* deducted two points for Samuel Banton's foul language."

Pax gulped and looked sideways at his roommate. Samuel had gone pale, his mouth hanging open. As the Judges realised they were no longer in the lead in the Polls, a huge cry of angst was met with huge roars of approval from the Loyals over on the other side of the chamber. They had just overtaken the Judges.

Pax leant towards Samuel and whispered. "Doesn't matter. The main thing is we saved the school, and didn't come last." But his roommate just stared at the floor, wringing his hands together.

"The review also revealed that Zachariah Thomson's front disc had been coated with a reflective paint," continued Miss Adams.

Another gasp filled the room.

"Therefore, I have decided to deduct ten points from the Loyals' score for such blatant cheating."

The scoreboard above Miss Adams' head flickered to darkness and then re-appeared, showing the final, adjusted tally. The Judges had won after all, and the Loyals were now in last place. This time there were cheers from three quarters of the room, totally drowning out the groans and cries from the Loyals. Pax paused for a moment, checking there weren't any more adjustments. When Miss Adams finally sat down, he leapt up and joined in the wild celebrations.

JUDGES	254
CHANCELLORS	253
PEERS	252
LOYALS	245

"Hah!" shouted Megan, over the screams and applause. "If we're lucky, Zachariah will get picked in the Draft and booted out of school."

"You're forgetting, he's exempt from the Draft 'cos he won the talent show," said Samuel bouncing up and down on the spot.

Pax looked across the room. All of the Loyals had turned their anger on Zachariah, pointing figures, shouting names. The big bully sat with his head hung low, motionless. Zachariah's popularity had at least suffered, even if they weren't getting rid of him this year.

[-]

When the friends got back to the Judges' common room, the celebrations began. Megan and Samuel got most of the plaudits for winning that final battle. Miss Adams had asked Pax and his friends to keep quiet about her treatment for some reason, so nobody knew what a vital role Pax had played in keeping the school open. But he didn't mind that. He was just pleased to be partying with his friends. Above the fireplace, in the middle of the mantelpiece, was a gleaming silver trophy. The engraving on the front said "Parliamentary Polls" and the handles at the side had been decorated with grey ribbons.

Nobody could remember the last time the Judges had won, but it was nice to look forward to next year's extra perks for winning the Polls. The third years would be graduating, of course, and thanks to this victory, their future prospects would be bright.

Everybody busied themselves packing their bags. There would be no-one from Judges staying here during the summer holidays except Pax and a few orphaned second years. He hung around the Central Lobby just like he had ten months earlier on that first day of school.

"See you, droid-boy," said Megan with a big grin on her face. She drew him into a big hug and this time, Pax hugged her back.

His cheeks flushed red as he spotted Briony with her bags. "I'll write to you," he finally managed to say after staring at the floor for a bit.

She kissed him on the cheek. "That would be nice."

Pax waved as the two girls left the building. He was just waiting for Samuel when Zachariah appeared, pulling a wheeled bag behind him. He stared at Pax in silence as he walked past. A summer full of workhouse-like duties awaited all the Loyals as punishment for coming last in the Polls.

For once, Zachariah looked the same size as everyone else, with his head bowed and shoulders slumped. There was no smile or hug waiting for him from his tall father.

"Thanks to your failure, the Loyals finished last," said Mr Thomson, not caring who heard. "I almost wish it had been your name drawn in the Draft."

"But Father, I won the talent show and the drone race. I came second in—"

"The least I would expect with the advantages you have. You cheated in the wargames and, what's worse, you got caught doing it! Honestly, I thought you were suitable material for the Council. Now, I'm not so sure."

"I'm sorry, Father. I will try harder next year, I promise."

Pax smiled at first, enjoying the bully getting a taste of his own medicine, but as the sermon continued at top volume and Zachariah shrank lower and lower, Pax began to feel sorry for him.

Finally, Samuel appeared. Pax tried to think of an excuse to keep him here for longer, but couldn't. School just wouldn't be the same without all his friends.

"You will keep in touch, won't you?" asked Pax.

"Course I will, whelk head! Ain't ever getting rid of me, now. Will try to sort out a summer picnic for you and the rest of the gang."

Pax smiled. *The gang*. He liked the sound of that.

Pax remained sitting in the lobby long after he had said goodbye to Samuel. No doubt the boys would swap messages on their wrist tabs as they worked their way through all the extra homework Miss Adams had given them.

But that was for another day. A butterfly fluttered upwards into the octagonal roof space of the lobby. Pax watched the delicate insect climb towards the sunbeams shining through the stained-glass windows. It was going to be a long and peaceful summer.

He reached inside his boiler suit and woke up Roacher, who scrambled onto his shoulder. "Come on. We've got repairs to do. Let's see if we can't get Bee-Bop up and running again, eh?"

ACKNOWLEDGEMENTS

First and foremost, I would like to thank James at Tiny Tree for believing in Pax's story and helping me bring it to life. Anthony, for championing my book. You guys work so tirelessly in the background to help authors like me realise their dreams. Catherine – thank you for sterling efforts during the editing process. You made this a better story and didn't make me cry once. Bruna – I love your cover!

When I made the switch to writing for a younger audience, I did so partly because the children's writing community is inclusive, supportive and fun. It has not disappointed. I joined SCBWI in 2018 and haven't looked back since. There are so many volunteers who help the society tick along, so many friendly faces and experienced authors willing to help. There are too many to mention by name.

Special thanks go to fellow members of the SCBWI Wokingham crit group. Anisah, Kat, Kim, Lorna, Mark, Philip, Sally P, Sally R, Sarah and Zoe, you guys are awesome! I love our monthly get togethers and your helpful feedback. You've kept me sane during this long journey.

To Dad, thanks for your cheerleading and support back in Cheshire. I wish Mum could have been here to read this one. And finally, to Fiona and Amelie, thank you for always being by my side throughout this roller coaster ride. Without quite breaking into a Bryan Adams song, everything I do…

ABOUT THE AUTHOR

David Barker started writing stories at school, got side-tracked by economics for twenty-five years, then re-discovered his love for writing when he attended the Faber Academy in 2014. His first book – a dystopian James Bond-esque thriller – turned into a trilogy by accident (The Gold Trilogy, Bloodhound Books).

He switched to children's fiction in 2018. Since then, he has written many stories, and dabbled with scriptwriting – including a Pantomime script for his local am-dram society (oh no he hasn't!). Pax & The Missing Head is the first in a new series.

He lives in Berkshire with his wife and daughter. He has a passion for stories (books and films), sport (especially tennis, golf and surfing) and boardgames (too many to mention). You can find out more at https://davidbarkerauthor.co.uk or follow him on Twitter @BlueGold201 or Instagram barker1397.